Spend It All

by
Todd Lazarski

**RED
GIANT
BOOKS**

for Paloma,
Nina,
Amelia,
and Scott Norwood

I spilled myself along the roads.
Mold grew on me as I dampened in alleys.
I began in ignorance. How could I know
that whoever is grinding up his soul is making
himself afresh? That the ones who run away
get nearer all the time? Look here or there,
it's always the horizon, the dull edge
of earth dicing your plan like a potato.

- Denis Johnson

AUTHOR'S NOTE

On January 3, 1993, despite semi-reliable kicker Scott Norwood having long ago been fed to the wolves, and despite legendary running back O.J. Simpson being long retired, comfortably-suited, leather-gloved, and microphone-wielding on the sideline, and with starting quarterback Jim Kelly slowed by a balky knee and all-pro running back Thurman Thomas similarly hobbled, the Buffalo Bills overcame a 35-3 third quarter deficit to defeat the Houston Oilers in an NFL Wild Card Playoff game.

Still to this day the single greatest comeback in NFL history, the so-called "Comeback Game" has become a treasured but mostly meaningless piece of scrap in the dustbin of football history, coming as it did amidst a four-year run of postseason failure, from 1990 through 1993, during which the Bills made it to, and lost, every Super Bowl.

Even so, of the beleaguered lot of people that shake their fists and hem and then haw and then sometimes moan over the exploits of the particular team that wears the agreed-upon colors of their respective hometown, Bills fans are especially infected. And many of these poor souls view the "Comeback Game" as, at worst, something like their own personal Super Bowl, or, at best, momentary proof of the existence of a benevolent, or at least sometimes-giving-a-shit, God.

Any narrative parallels drawn from the story that follows and the "Comeback Game," metaphoric or otherwise, are strictly coincidental. Such happy endings belie the condition, all conditions, of living.

PROLOGUE

Had I mentioned the real intention behind my return home—eating myself to death—I'm pretty sure my grandmother's reaction may have been more subdued. Hard to tell, what with the sheer bursting nature of grandmotherly inertia, once it gets going, like a cat sensing an impending human hand to the head, and the sight of me always enough to set her over the percolation point anyway. Regardless of my current financial status, state of employment, or ceaseless need for her to retrieve the clutch from her dresser, dig into the seeming endless stack of twenty-dollar-bills therein, and pull out another to be used in support of my cheesesteak habit (her imploring all the while, "don't spend it *all*"), it's always the same. She forgets all the requisite pent-up bitterness and cynicism that mark the decline into old, old age, the sliding down the hallway of funerals and forgetfulness and doctor appointments and stuffy-housed waiting and arthritis, and getting her flabby, drooping arms around her youngest grandson is an act of last purity, of unequivocal deliverance. Even if sometimes, usually, almost always, I do spend it all.

The manipulation of the soft-and-big-hearted game, I know it well, and most around me, Grandma included, know that I know it well. My cat, hovering between rooms, stopping now to devotedly lick his own asshole, even this benign beast knows the score. So when I make the call, flipping channels aimlessly, settling into a good ass-groove on the couch, the loquacious dreamer poet stance I picture when I'm being generous toward myself, which I often am, and you never can tell how long these talks might go, I only half-hint at the quarter-assigned writing assignment and flippantly ignore the semi-veiled inquiry about my fiancé. I don't even let the fact that Grandma uses the word "fiancé" for the first time, ever, throw me. Darting back and forth between the NFL and Food Networks, I run through the usual checklist: ask about her knee, deflect questions about my "book," occasionally politely space out with a "yeahhh..." The game plan is a simple pep talk to stoke her enthusiasm enough so that, next time, we can skip the plate-setting rigmarole and she'll know immediately what I'm referring to with the 300-some buck request.

The plane ticket, Grandma, plaaain-ehh–yes, they are expensive.

I hint at least four times that I'll be there for awhile, and I catch myself balling my non-phone hand into a frustrated furious-fist each time the conversation turns back to the weather, which it does, inevitably, frequently.

"Yeah," I say, "fucking landlord hasn't even turned on the heat yet."

"Ohhh... Teddy..."

In boxing this might be known as a double-punch, unfair, grounds for immediate forfeiture, a blatantly unnecessary F-bomb teamed with news that I'll be dead of hypothermia by the end of the weekend. But she asks for it, and takes it, nearly every time the weather turns cold. As it is now, as we speak, as I'm kicking around the shadowy Bucktown apartment that passes, I think, still, maybe, as a token of substantial post-college success. A place of my *own*, only not quite, of course, because who can afford a place of their own? So there is Smoke, and that near constant ashtray smell that used to only hang over the coffee table but by this point has seeped into the everyday breath of the abode, even when he's not around.

"Well, you should probably come over, then," she says.

"What you got the heat at, Grandma? 76?"

"Yeah, I think so, let me check..."

I picture the waddling, in those old plastic-y Grandmother slip-on slippers toward the thermostat. It's barely mid-November and most of the East Coast is still awaiting the first real snow of the season. Football season has barely parted her thighs, so it feels, and

Helka Rawski is already contemplating the icicle-like nature of the doorknobs on her tiny suburban bungalow, which reminds me to maybe second and third guess what I'm throwing myself into here.

"I'll keep it however high you want," she assures me. "Should I turn it up? I'll turn it up."

"Grandma, fuck, you ever hear of *room* temperature!?"

I'm not sure how it will play out with the newspaper, the approvals and the deadlines and that old editor who's barely older than me; or with my book, ridiculous and overwrought, lost in a kind of grayish limbo query purgatory; or with big Smoke, and the matter of rent; or with that certain person whose new title is hard for me to comprehend, hard for Grandma to comprehend, seeing as how I'm barely or even not at all old enough to fuck. I remember how I told her:

"Grandma, so, I'm uh, en, *engaged*…"

"Oh, Teddy! Teddy, Teddy, that's great. But, Teddy, you're not old enough."

"Grandma, I am too old enough! I'm old enough to fuck!"

How we had laughed, the F-word, that *other* F-word, and I. And now, lately, for some or another reason—the coming holidays, the global warming, the economic climate, any of the litany of things-to-blame-other-things-on—I hardly feel like calling her back.

I also think about the non-assignment, the one not yet approved, the one in my head, the one itching the edges of my fingers, and my intestines. I think, and wonder, on the pizza, the *hometown* pizza, the pepperoni and their grease pools, and the fire-sauced, hemorrhoid-yielding chicken wings, the very foodstuffs that maybe, if I'm hero enough, will end me once and for all.

"Oh - what should we do?" Helka asks, probably clasping her hands together, just boiling now, her little water bubbles shooting furiously to the surface.

"Gonna be a lot of eating. Maybe more than normal."

"Oh, with your *ulcer*? Well, do what you have to do. Are they going to pay you this time?"

As a professional, at least mostly-professional, journalist, this is not a comment to be dignified, nor should it be suffered by a highly-esteemed grandson. Possibly the most highly esteemed of the two.

"I'll turn down the beds," she says.

"Christ, shit, I don't even have a ticket yet..."

"Oh, the *language*."

"And I don't know why I can't just sleep with you."

So different than how I thought it would be. So much less sexy than the description I heard tumbling out of my lips last night at the bar, a classy but not-showing-off Four Roses in hand, humble-bragging my way into the bartender's only half-questioning eyes, him looking to see if there was someone less drunk to help as I described a "food and culture travelogue," just until "the book is finished up," "edited," and "I'm done shopping it around." He mostly just wanted to know if I'd have another, now I'd tilted my head, poetic-like, and let the rocks slide from the bottom of the glass to kiss my lips. I would.

"Teddy, I'm turning the guest bed down. You'll be comfortable. And I can *still* scratch your back in there."

How I had fantasized so much else, so much *more*, exposed brick condos and a power-locking car I'd importantly strut toward every morning with steaming travel mug of coffee in hand, medical residencies or some such thing, important paperwork in manila folders, hustling to and fro out of an elevator, wearing barely-loosened ties in a sleek modern office with a ping-pong table and an espresso machine in the break room, where a girl in a skirt smiles at me with her eyes, but we're really just great work friends. She understands me and has great calves, and there we are together in the not-tired downtown of a notable city, a city with a subway even, and a reputable happy hour bar around the corner where cronies always want to buy me one, and to hear my story about how I won that impossible case, got the scoop, finalized the sale—*even though I don't speak Arabic*! I indulge them, regale all my co-workers, these hungry masses around me as though at the feet of Christ, or someone else real Boss-like, with tales of triumph and days of victory while the barkeep wipes down the fancy oak with a towel and shakes his head with impressed *thought I'd heard it all* disbelief.

"*Teddy, Teddy! Tell the one again 'bout the cow convention in Des Moines!*"

"*Aaaaagh, I heard this one!*"

"*Yeah, yeah.*"

Someone getting excited, me turning toward them with rocks glass in hand, sleeves rolled up, stoic but mischievous, calming my elated audience with arms out in acquiescence, pleading for calm before the anecdotal masterpiece. The girl with the calves sits towards the back of the rapt circle and looks up with a grin, her eyelashes doing that thing that certain big city 20-somethings learn to do when new to the professional world, especially when daily in the presence of someone full of grizzled life experience and the subsequent grandiose wisdom.

"*What about that arm-wrestling contest in Istanbul, Teddy? You son of a bitch! Jimmy ya hear 'dat one!?*"

And when it's over I return home, after a hearty pat on the back from the boss, to the honey. She went to Vassar, or one of those vaguely New England-ish schools—she's never a snob about it—and became a public defender or a school teacher, or a nurse, she loves helping people. She also loves making me great meals—Laotian, Cambodian, some far off part of the world we'll one day visit, her scrunching eyebrows over a rice-and-turmeric-centric cookbook—but not tonight. She's there when I walk in, sitting cross-legged on the leather couch pushed back against said exposed brick, reading something deep that I've already read, and I smile to myself, professorially.

"Oh, you're reading Chekhov!"

Monk or Richie Havens or something Western African, cultural and laid back, plays low in the background, and she smiles over her glasses as I walk through the door, me now fully loosening the tie, dropping the briefcase, her rising to greet her king, panties moistening appropriately as the fire, the roaring cinematic background kind, licks and dances to its ceaseless crackle, our dinner reservations—*"Let's just go out tonight, baby." "Oh, Teddy, really!? Can we?" "Of course we can, you, look at you, you deserve it"* —the only remaining unknown.

So different than how I had foreseen the approach to my 30th birthday, 30 always so far off, far enough that there was time for the procurement of all these things. Starting, maybe, tomorrow; or next week, latest. Always starting and stopping, the checklist in my mind, *OK, the office has to be sleek...*

Instead there are things like, well, my grandmother, alive and kicking, her tricep flab still jiggle-jiggling as she pokes at something fatty and delicious in a pan on the translucent brown-stained stove. She still answers my calls, and this is important, I tell myself, by now absent-mindedly scratching nuts between the pajama pants and boxers, more engrossed in the top 10 plays of last Sunday— that fucking catch!—than focused on the device stuck to my ear or the runaway train of grandma-thought. But, yes, some face time with a great influence, or, well, an influence, on my life, before I stuff myself to the point of not moving, permanently. A grand return home, to my roots, ahead of asphyxiation by burrito, and leaving that near-polished book and some notes on my hometown as my grand legacy.

There's also some 6K in credit card debt, and the befuddled gaggle of fiancé, cat, and Smoke, the trio left behind to sort out the remnants and split the 180 and change in my checking account. I'll leave it to them to make empty promises to one another to get somebody to polish and publish my manuscript, to make promises so far as to *read* said manuscript—double-spaced and sitting on the floor next to the laptop desk, underneath a cold, mostly-empty coffee cup and the stolid, tortured eyes of cartoon Kerouac on the wall. I'll be away from it all, tragically, after heroically stuffing the face hole, damning all known ulcers, breathing deep my own flatus, sitting back in stuffed chairs that protest my very presence, joining the Fat Fuck Hall of Fame.

And so it is that I turn my collar up to the cooling Chicago early-winter air, away from the under-radiator dust bunnies, our respectable stereo, the speakers with no place to sit but on the floor, toward the place of my conception, and my kicking-dragging departure from the cool dreams and warm vibes of my mother's cozy womb into the blizzard swirls and blows and asskicks of Buffalo.

1. BUFFALO

The hero's journey, beginning…

Like so many with a cab ride, with the unspoken contract that I have money and will pay before darting out of the car, into traffic, not waiting for my destination, just going, and the driver always thinking I'm not fast enough, and me always thinking maybe he's not, I hold a 20 and a 10 in my hand, and we're in agreement on the destination with a shared language still, always, in silent compromise.

Ok, you can rap endlessly and loudly in your bluetooth in, eh, what is that, Morroccan? Long as you end up at O'Hare.

And I shall try to say a couple words in English, whilst not killing us both under the weight of a semi-truck, so long as you tip me, of course.

"Airport, yes?"

"Oh. Hair."

And off we go, the running the other way slot machine of my adopted city working through the window. It all takes on that dramatic last scene scope, the string-section swelling, a denouement montage imminent, the way leaving home always sounds. My neighborhood segues gradually into the next, the alleys looking like infinite garbage can-dotted hallways extending toward a brick-lined life you might consider chasing when you only get that half-second, speeding-by glimpse.

But like the business-suiters around me at the airport drop-off, zigging and zagging, hopping in and out of cabs, charcoal sport jackets and such over beefy shoulders shouldering leather-cased laptops, assured in their slicked back hair and neatly-trimmed goatees, a Big Ten diploma and a childhood of eating corn leading to this life of meetings, hotels, flights, *this isn't so bad,* I think, and pay my Moroccan sprinter friend, shoulder my rucksack, and lean generally toward motion.

Yep - ain't doing so bad my own self, fellas, got a bed waiting for me, after all, a plane's ride away, sure, yep I fly all the time too and it don't bother me none, neither, no prob, just like you, yeah, musta forgot my sport jacket though, eh?... EH? With an elbow nudge.

It's like they generously let a little brother step into their pickup game when I sidle into a generic Terminal C bar in my Bills knit cap and splotchy sideburns. I get carded and lightly scoffed at when the guy with glasses and a ruddy drinker's face sipping a sidecar or some such old guy drink spies the emblem adorning the side of my hat. Ever the Sportsmanship Award winner, I smile politely, gaze down, give him his victory and concede my silly otherness. Even without vocal mention of the Bears, the whole thing is hopelessly like the late-night comedy sketch, and I wonder if yokels ever tire of their existence as yokels. But Goose Islands are to be drank, and the severity of TSA and the cutting edge massiveness of the whole thing spitting and sucking persons to all corners of the earth is meant to be softened. The business travelers are to be suffered, it all research, maybe, into how things shouldn't go down.

I drink two beers and think about the trip.

No matter what, I remind myself, each swallow it gets easier, I'm less than two quarter-drunk hours from that great adult experience: the airport pickup. You've survived, and are someplace new, or old, or far, and have been given a new lease on life. Supplied with hard-won wrinkles in your corduroy's fanny region, you are the brave earner of fresh adventure tales. You've arrived at the distant nether regions of the land outside baggage claim sliding doors, where cigarettes have never tasted so good and standing outside, even in Buffalo fall air, hoping for a glimpse of your grandmother's Malibu, feels like a great emancipation. You look around, and the future opens up, the diagnosis is benign, and so you smoke another. In the drama of flying, the airport itself, all multifaceted signage and corridors, directional possibilities and echoing bathrooms, seems exciting. Even the Buffalo airport—clean, pristine, nearly *in-*

ternational-feeling—is bolstered by its existence as agent in a wildly successful collaboration, bringing me down out of the sky, slowing me, channeling me through that rushing churning wildness, into a terminal that reeks wonderfully of chicken wing sauce. Just like that, it's the old groove, and wait...is that...new oil for the fryer? Especially for my arrival?

We heard you were coming.

It's in the bartender's eyes, and, ride en route or not, I'll have plenty of time to down a Labatt's and a shot of Jamo, not even sitting, just propping my elbows on the wood to air out my post-flight sweaty pits before leaning into the night. I hold off on ordering wings like a man bent on serious, special-night foreplay, on making it last.

It feels good to be home.

All this awaits, I know, as we take off in Chicago, and I can picture it: my brother pulling up in our grandmother's borrowed ride, the Top or some such business blaring on the stereo about women, or cars, or cars as women in metaphor, him looking a bit heavier and balder under his cap, a Camel in lips he ashes out a quarter-cracked window. His "Whatsuup!?" exaggerated, upbeat, his nod the same as my nod, coming as it does from some primordial goo-ish place back beyond our control or understanding, back from when our father's father's father was picking up siblings from the airport as an excuse to leave the house and a reason to get irresponsibly twisted. And yes, it's a bit infectious, like crabs, enough so that, inevitably, we'll end up at some house, drunkenly flopping, when what I want, always want, is spicy burritos and Grandma's recliner, her gently browbeating the world-weary Magellan now prostrate before her, his stinky holey socks pointing out toward the TV—"Oh, O'Hare!??"—impressed and dropping a twenty for my late night stroll thru the Mighty Taco drive-thru.

Good sport that I am, that one must become on night number

one, when arms have been opened and plans have been changed, cars borrowed and flight times noted, I cede to the whiskey route. Allentown might as well be Greenwich Village, and the macabre stick figure in front of Gabriels' Gate the Eiffel Tower. We'll have wings, obviously, but first we'll drink in of that far away bar time, Bills neon lights endless around us and heads getting obscure, a post-flight buzz always coming so easy. I'll blame the altitude change, as is my way, and we'll head to Frizzy's for another Maker's. We'll drink like, on night one anyways, it seems only brothers can, 'member-when-ing and laying plans for the future within the same exhale of moonlit Camel smoke. We'll walk into a joint at some point later and "1984" or "Golden Years," something bass-y and fast, will be bumping, and there will be chicks atop the bar, everybody clasping each other on the back, and we'll hit the front door like those old swinging wooden half-door jobs from a wild west saloon, and the blonde with the bandana gyrating lustily will spot my Bills logo hat and point and immediately gush, and there will be a general whirring buzz, and we'll walk through the room in slow-motion, everybody high-fiving and shaking hands with us, leaving conversations to turn and smile and greet and offer a drink on their tab. Girls with their googly eyes, blushing, will offer "welcome homes," and we'll become the beloved outlaws, back, finally, from an undeserved stint at Rikers, a long tour of noble duty, a brave, non-maligned hour-plus flight from Chicago.

Really, though, it'll mostly be some corner stools and the soft clink of Molson bottles, a beer-gutted, smokers-growl bartender with an attitude, and awkward, quiet pauses between Dire Straits jams on the juke. Either way, we'll stroll Allen and Virginia, and other street names Chicago can't claim, and wind up on a couch each at John's old friend's place, his former bass player now a successful adult, house-owner. Unwashed and off the grid, phone calls will remain unreturned, Grandma, as is her sad plot, left waiting, and wondering, as she should, if we need a ride home from the bar. We forget to remember to call her, and she forgets that we already have her car.

It sprawls before me in hazy foresightedness, as it's occurred before, at the start of the interminable O'Hare runway taxi. I fiddle with the plastic orb above my seat that brings air, for something, anything to do with my glistening hands, the cool air chilly on the palms. I rub them on my cords and search for something to read behind the barf bag in the seat in front of me, feeling my body turn with the wheels of the big bird, things out of my control now, something has been set in motion, a feigned heart attack or overloud usage of a phrase containing the word "bomb" in it all that can halt the action, and I currently have the balls for neither.

2. CHICAGO (0-1)

Even for the Bills, my Bills, the victorious squad of my youth and the legion of pummeling folly in near-adulthood, there's that point in every season, like that of the breathy whispers of a Tim Robbins character, when hope is real. Like the fetus before the extra chromosome reveal, or the tweener before the pubescent dreamy waywardness and sticky sheets, or the moment just prior to the Goth teenage phase of willful misanthropy and black nail polish, when it becomes evident to even the most loving parents that potential has been squandered and mediocrity is the official best case scenario, such it is that I rise through the cobwebs and cottonmouth of a particularly rough September hangover. I brush my teeth and don a Thurman Thomas t-shirt jersey that's been laid over my hardwork writing chair for the past week—laying out shirts my own particular method of fabric smoothing, I've yet to master the iron, nor know where or how to procure an ironing board—and head to the one sports bar in my decidedly non-sports-ish neighborhood.

Smoke will sit this one out, he informs me, smirking as he slumps Sunday-foggily on the couch. Shrugging my shoulders, all non-committal but already putting on my boots, I make it evident that it's whatever—*whatever, fuckers*, I mean—I have neither the time nor inclination to deal with non-believers, to deal with fans of the team based here in town, mere miles away, and their infected self-centeredness, their solipsistic hometown-ness, like it's a Springsteen song and all other realities, fan bases, dreams and desperate disappointments, are non-factors. It's Sunday, the season is infantile, and I have but freshman optimism for the possibilities of my guys.

"Fred Jackson, *fuckers!*" I hear myself shouting repeatedly in my head, shaking a fist, shocking the county, as they say, and scoffing at friends, at staggering Smoke and his smug *don't need to go out to see my team*, stagnating all the faithless teleprompting analysts while serving notice to big Chicago and its self-satisfied shoulders, quieting all those agnostic stat-wielders. Really showing that girl from high school, and that other one too, with her head shake and forever moving away from me in the lunchroom of my mind. It's what I imagine morning people feel like when waking—the sense of opportunity, the arms-outstretched freshness and clean-slate glory of that impending first cup of coffee, or the snap of the top of an alcoholic's new vodka bottle, whatever the case: they rarely realize it's all just a momentary lack of strife, forthcoming tiredness as inevitable as near-empty cups of cold caffeine, stifled yawns, headaches.

I stroll now, turning south into the gray fall air. A part of me, inside, somewhere near the intestines, hopes the Bills will stink by the time the wind on Milwaukee Avenue turns truly cold, so I won't feel the need to get out of warm Sunday hangover blankets. I already miss Sunday sleep-ins, and the season is still so young, but the feeling passes quickly, followed immediately by a secret, metaphoric punch to the throat, and I turn my stroll into a strut. Because, well, goddamn, it just takes a lean, and some pace, and, just, *godddamnit!* Early September is no time for loser talk, and so I put my hands in my pockets, deep, magnanimously, let the armpits build a healthy, anticipatory glisten, and march along like a man with chesty direction, a man late for the overdue punishment of a stepchild, leaving the Camel dangling by itself, my lips can handle the smoke-work. Suddenly I look quite the fearless strutting badass, especially for a cheerer of a team currently sitting at 0-1.

Ten minutes later I'm at the bar, rubbing my hands together, cupping them and blowing warm air in, clapping lightly, nodding my head, finding my role. I wind-mill my arms a bit now, getting set, loose, high-kneeing in place, ordering a Bloody, getting ready for the usual disbelief:

"You want to watch *what* team?"

It's rather hard to find a decent nesting spot, one of comfort and some understanding, let alone the mutual loser camaraderie that comes from simpatico souls in AA meetings, dentist waiting rooms, or Detroit. Buffalo produces the same, but it's especially difficult to find in Chicago butthead territory, where the gameday blue and orange evokes deeper voices and macho bullishness, skewed and bad-tasting, even when pitched with a comedic bent. It helps none when your squad has fallen the way of the pager, laughable, a token of out-of-place kitsch, *Aww, look!* Irrelevant is the term most of those around me would use, if they even found the time to talk about the Bills, if the Old Style-swilling Ditka-dom had bankroll room for any consideration paid toward that other conference.

"Oh, I think he's watching it down there," the bartender says, and points, right before dropping the floppy pickle down into my red-filled glass.

Only later, looking back, will I insert the proper gravitas, only with nostalgic hindsight will I get the booming serendipity of it all. The bartender, oblivious, pointing out the obvious, playing the unknown connector of lost souls, the traffic light that fritzes one second for that fateful collision, altering two courses, shattering windshields and opening eyes wide while causing extensive, inalterable body damage. But for now, flipping her my debit card, all I can muster is, "Wait, what?"

And there he is, his back to me, his neck craned toward a corner TV in a forgotten, cobwebbed nook of the joint. Looking back on it, it seems that the music stopped, that everything around me in the bar entered slow-motion. That the *Simpson 32* on the back of his shirt emerged from a sea-parting moment where a beefcake in an Urlacher jersey bent down to check his phone and the chick in the low-cut Cutler shirt swiveled her stool 180 degrees to order another Lite and the always-present Packers dickhead, just looking for trouble, for a bloody nose, to prove his cock-length, moved towards the men's room.

These moments that play back just so have always been a minor obsession. Like "Jumpin' Jack Flash" with a Scorsese slow-pan, there it is, there's me: buying beer for the first time with a fake ID that says I'm a redheaded 220-pounder from Michigan, which I am, I tell myself, turning with the case of Busch toward the counter man at the off-campus quickie mart who's already eying me, everything slowing down into before-and-after life magnitude; and there's me again, popping, rather maliciously detonating, my cherry in the back seat of Ma's car, Ma ignorant at home, knitting, probably, by an old time stove fireplace while I'm parked in a dark corner of a parking lot with requisite stereotypical nerves and Zeppelin 2 playing on repeat; and there's little me, eyes closed, as Scott Norwood lines everything up, the laces, yes, but also the thrust of my then seven-year-old life, and missing, ensuring the coming demise of my old man, not to mention kick-starting my future all-consuming need for booze and fatty food comfort-seeking, and my penchant to flee, to always need to go outside, to smoke endlessly, to stare at the stars and wonder on everything that might have been.

But this is adulthood, this is a lazy Sunday, this is supposed to be the slow, sad dragging-out of yet another in a series of lost weekends, team spirit shown because it's a socially acceptable reason to get smashed on Sunday afternoon and eat goopy nachos, because this is what you do, and nothing more. Regardless, I walk over, note the faded nature of the blue on his Simpson jersey, it's got some age, he's not some bandwagon homicide fan, not some closet misogynist that thinks enough time has passed where it'd be a riot to wear this jersey, the ultimate societal-flaunt, a true fuck-you to every passing face with even a fleeting knowledge of '90's current events.

"Whaddyou? 'Skins fan?" he asks, half-turning from the tube's turned-down pre-game banter, taking note that I'm putting my glass down on the half-table in front of him and sizing him up, scrunching my eyebrows, taking it all in for later late-night contemplation.

"Nawww…" I say, and unzip my hoodie, a smirk forming, a weird anxiety, *a will she like it? Of course she'll like it.* Ceaseless self-doubt in there too, because *life is all disappointment and you thought Norwood had that kick and also that God loved you so you'd go on to have a condo in a big city and wear a tie to a nice sleek place of employment…*

Once upon a time, making new friends was a kind of concrete activity. "Mom, I made a new friend today, his name is Ricky." That actually happened, this a phrase I distinctly recall dropping one after-school ride home from second grade. As if it was consummated, as if there was no question. As if I were saying, "Mom, *I fucked Ricky,*" there little doubt as to the actual hurdle cleared, to the hymen being broken. *There was penetration, Mom.* When did it become like this, difficult—eccentric, even—to talk to people, and weirder still to give your number to a stranger, harder to avoid hanging out only with the people you happen to share an office with, simply because you share an office with them and it just makes things easier, and so damn-near impossible for a chance, single-serving buddy you talked to at a bar because he was wearing a Grateful Dead t-shirt to become anything more lasting than that?

But sometimes you find yourself pushing through, stiff-arming 30-year-old complacency and shaking hands with a 6'4 totem of hardwired football energy in an OJ Simpson jersey. A man from Dunkirk—just outside Buffalo, or "a Jim Kelly throw from Buffalo," as he will later put it—swilling Labatt's, which they don't have on the beer list here, and booming with laughter, assured, derisive of those around us not wearing Bills garb, which is everybody, nodding emphatically with familiar, happy knowledge at your mention of Tonawanda. He offers his hand again, shakes his head in disbelief, puts his hands on the table and juts up his jaw ponderously before bellowing, *"Tonawandaaaah!?"* He drags out the name of my home suburb, and when he does it's like how you feel when a songwriter mentions a place you've been in a song. He says it again, and I'm nodding, and maybe even blushing, butterflies cracking open their cocoons in my stomach, and now he's asking if I like whiskey.

Dustin has sandy blonde hair and an impossibly rumbling, of-the-gut voice, especially on every Bills sack and first down, and after hard-fought Fred Jackson 4-yard runs, when we collectively break into a chorus of *"Fredddieee"* accompanied by double fist pumps that downshift into a high-five and pat on the back and another murmur of whiskey. Especially, too, when he's ordering me a shot, simultaneously annoying and charming the bartender, her initially unsure and then smirking, threatened then surprised, then smitten, having never seen something like this before, something so silly and so serious on a rote Sunday of NFL white noise and daytime-drunk tips. At least not since last week.

"This is our spot," he informs me. He took in week 1's loss here and tells me we'll take in "no more," and with this he belts out a laugh, and a belch squeaks out with it, and for me something slips away and I feel miles from Smoke and everyone that laughed at my Sunday plans last night.

You're going where, *to watch* who?

Dustin has begun throwing his own flags, not metaphorically, literally, at one point whipping a yellow beanie against the nearest wall for a missed holding call. I eventually get up to get it for him, smiling strangely, shrugging, jogging back to our table, shaking my head.

Sometimes the Bills look good. Better than good. Rolling. Heaven-sent, or some such inexplicable thing that poets drone on and on about, the verses getting away from them, running toward prose, though they're careful, knowing that would be too much of a commitment, too much admittance that they don't know what the hell is the difference between the this and the that. Something just this side of obscure, obtuse, but the stars are aligning, to borrow their—one of their—phrases. Like the checkout man accepting fake proof of ID to grant my 18-year-old dreams; like the backseat goddess and her too-generous, barely-earned leg-part moan; like the goalposts of Super Bowl 25 that taught me life's surest lesson: it doesn't make sense how it all works. Like a machine, how my miming over-the-shoulder catches, followed with a quick spin move, becomes acceptable public behavior, Dustin doing the same, showing me Thurman in the '91 Divisional Playoff game, quick shuffling his feet, "Remember his eyes in slow-mo!?" he shouts, and shows me wide eyes, stutter-stepping, seeing the hole, "then Bam!" and he stops to swill from his High Life bottle.

We're 'member-when-ing and he's pushing up the sleeves on his shirt and saying "Damn, Tonawandaaah!?" and shaking his head. I notice how he rests both hands, in anticipation, on his stool before every 3rd down, willing a conversion, leaning in. The Bills are winning and I've had three Bloodies and three Jameson shots by the start of the 3rd, we've already exchanged numbers by the time I step outside for my second smoke of the day, Dustin joining, us with a sideways glance at one another and a little-kid giggle, one quick pat on the back as he holds open the door for me. The fall has opened up like the greatest morning with the best coffee in the history of Columbia, Ethiopia, wherever. I even make note to call my mother and tell her the news, after the big Bills win.

3. JIM'S STEAKOUT
2180 Sheridan Dr.
Buffalo, NY, 14223

As is the way with editors—those insipid correctors, condescenders, hall-monitors of art and soul—mine has a lot to learn about life. And journalism. Namely, primarily, the essential fact that no one can write about food.

Is there garlic in this? I think there's some garlic in this. I really like how they did the garlic in this. Do you think they diced it? I think they may have roasted it whole! Holy fuck! They put this motherfucking head of garlic in the goddamn oven with the heat on! Who woulda thought to do that? I am just balled the fuck over...

My contributions to the collective understanding of human existence and society to this point have been approximately so, and these insights continue, in 33-cents-per-word increments, all the way to the bar, to happy hour, until that long-sought, finally realized utterance of mine achieves reality, *I'm a writer,* and the bartender pours another whiskey and we both know our roles and laugh, and ignore the destruction of healthy consciousness by our respective poisons and bullshit.

Jim's epitomizes the difficulty in literarily dissecting caloric intake, or at least of doing so without the appropriate, stupid, Proustian flights of Romantic era—or whatever era that is—poetic fancy. How else could one describe what happens with the cheese, the melting, the liquefying, and it all taking place within the nooks, the topographical map textures, the crags and caverned recesses, of scrappy meat? Ribeye, so they say, is diced in those little scraggly ribbons of thin cowiness, and the crisp-ended tenderness is sensual, inducing the kind of bites of a baby that hasn't yet learned to use its hands, just leaning at the middle, needing the mouth on the thing, now.

The construction is where everything consummates, the blueprint of a disappointed life assuaged, where the hammer-like miracle of breaded meat and cheese takes its glorious, greasy final form. The metaphor about the parts and the sum and the whole that I can never remember or understand. A favorite of food writers-slash-con men. But why is it always, mandatory it seems, a 17-year-old laboring and chiseling away back there, piling a heaping mound of brown dead cow atop the flattop? It's easy to wonder if the establishment is breaking some kind of labor law, and to almost feel a bit bad about it for a second, as if you are complicit in this kid's meager wages and bad skin. And why do you always want to look away, as if bearing witness will somehow negate the behind-the-scenes magic? It's right there in front of you, sizzling seductively, all *look-at-me* and *you hungry baby?* and *I'm gonna be all up in your mouth* and such, and you look, you must. This is certainly no time for disinterested charm, because this is also where it gets valiant: the cheese, added at just the right time. And how could one know? What kind of academy or culinary institute, or cheese-product YouTube tutorial, could school a willing teen in the art of getting the stuff to spread out, and over, and *through*?

How, also, to talk about how the first six inches treat a drunken appetite? Like a bouncer with PTSD who just found out he didn't get into the Academy. Full of steroids and Red Bull and veiny-bicep static. At this point there's already guilt about thoughts of the second half, a notion of *perhaps I should bring the rest home for Grandma.* Be kind, wait five minutes, be sane and sober about calories and how late it is. Or, if not for Grandma, wrap it up and throw it in the fridge for tomorrow's post-dump breakfast. Be reasonable, in any event—but the moment passes, like a drunk's minute of stupid clarity, post-drink, where the bartender is friendly and helpful and the light is low and the mood is right and he merely raises his eyebrows, questioning, cordial, and there's no denying the universe's occasional good grace, you'd hate to be the one to let him down, to give up your seat and let someone else take your cozy warm-dreams corner of the world, where you belong, after all, and before you know it you're pushing your sleeves back up, grabbing another paper napkin, lowering your jaw and face simultaneously, closer to the table, getting that corner bite with the mayo and the precariously-hanging banana pepper.

This is why it's a to-go sandwich, and part of the why of how my pieces often turn into instructionals. How I often want to take a reader by the ignorant shoulders, gently scolding, turning, guiding, step-dad-ish, no, no, *listen. It's how you play the game that counts*, or some such business. How I want to yell, but restrain myself, over the keyboard, nudging, pleading instead: take the bag, get back to the couch, stick your elbows out over the coffee table, and lean forward. Probably take off your pants first, then, look to the baby, as the key is to bring face to sandwich, and not vice versa. *Cheers*, Bills loss highlights, a late-night laugh-tracked suit, with a punchable smile—it doesn't matter what's on TV, because maintaining structural integrity will absorb nearly all focus. Overzealous handsiness leads to backend fallout. Don't squeeze. No, no the *guide hand*, is for, well, it's called the guide hand after all. Me, rustling my red-headed stepson's hair, right after he blows a conference semifinal at the charity stripe. Of course, fries are good for scooping up remnants, creating a makeshift dessert in the process, but *you can't start with dessert, you silly bastard knucklehead…*

I tried to explain all this once, on a similar post-college research foray, something like what some call a sabbatical, to a Tonawanda high school girl that caught my eye, snacking on fries as she was, and me so caught up in the euphoria, with first tongue penetrations on a dripping 'deluxe' steak hoagie ('Deluxe' being key, what you have to order, as it hints at something Chevy-ish, chrome and polished, sleek and high performance, with a 'turbo' maybe. What, in the tumbling drunken rationality of several hours of heroic drinking at Caputi's, I deserve). In hindsight, I should have stuck to my constant strive for benign, wordless charm, it didn't come off exactly right.

"The cheese! Eh? The way they melt the cheese..." I said, my mouth half-full, hot sauce on chin whiskers, a scrunched-up napkin in the palm, pointing with a pinky finger toward the meat mess on the table in front of me, as if it were a bodily exclamation point. And then back into it, head down, the focused hunch of a fat man at a foreign vending machine, shoulders sagging, the world washing away, now contented oblivion swishing, firing from oil-piqued salivary glands.

Jim's is a neon-lit joint on Sheridan, and we share the same birth year, as well as the same hours. It's far more than a stop on the walk from the bar back to Grandma's, much more like the reason to go to Caputi's at all—to withstand the bad jams, to waste a buck on one Zeppelin and two Stones songs, to hopelessly try to change their minds, to build and maintain a buzz. To have one more, punishing yourself, really, when you can hear the stomach churning and mere enjoyers of food would acquiesce, give in to the basic notion of, "I'm hungry, now." But the lonely chap in the Bills cap, no, not him, the other one, the one with the faraway smile, the one intent on chasing it all the way and getting the most possible run out of this night's hunger potential, the one that will order three beef tacos, hot, aside his 12-inch hoagie, first he'll have another Molson. Savoring, salivating, checking the menu on his phone but it's already in his head: it's all a bit much to explain, this affair, and it certainly has kept Grandma up on more than a few nights. Given her cause for a few rosaries, to wonder if she should hop in the Malibu in her nightgown and roll across Sheridan to pick me up. Force me to get a 6-inch, like a sensible being, a reasonable body-watcher, a snack that won't necessitate her banging on the bathroom door tomorrow morning, as she desperately wonders if everything is ok with my "paperwork."

"Teddy!? Ted, you fall in!?"

"So much paperwork, Grandma. Boss is really on my ass."

The indescribability of this all offers no excuse as to why the man with the glasses back home, possessor of the divine right of validation, hasn't confirmed my travelogue idea, agreed to a deadline, or said for sure whether it'll be published, I'll be paid. My professionalism, my degree, my loving, grease-logged pitch notwithstanding, these are words that, impossible or not, deserve to be sought. The magic is still, always, in the chasing, in the abstaining and then the gluttonous, parallel-to-the-ground tackling, all at once, of everything. A blitz of grand scheming, ballsy and clutch and other sports-y descriptors. Empty the secondary, send everyone. Put all the chips down, or up, or whatever may be the proper card game metaphor. Grandma's twenty has a chance of maintaining some life—for about one-and-a-half beers, though part of Jim's magic is also in the 5AM bed time.

And again, that's mere description, a number followed by some Latin letters. It is a closing-time question to ask Google or the semi-fat guy in the Bills hat at the bar, no, not him, the other one, he'll know. They both do.

You have to consider the sleepy, shades-drawn Tonawanda setting to get the incalculability in full-flavored context. How it doesn't add up. How you can almost approach what Proust was thinking, what he was smoking.

How many Molson Canadians it might take for him to abandon any inkling of bringing his grandmother six inches of ribeye and melted American-ish cheese and peppers and slathered spurty mayo...

Marcel, you didn't bring me a cheesesteak, sweetie, did you forget?

Grandma, fuck, I got like 800 pages to write today, get off my dick.

Jeez, 800. He sure goes on and on with the food talk, this last part to herself, under her breath, shuffling in her Frenchy slippers back toward the kitchen to see what else she can put in her sad, empty stomach.

Even for novelists, or for manuscriptists like me, the ones worthy of an answer for sent queries, for journalists respectable enough that the editor hit the 'Reply' button, occasionally, there's no describing the groove of crossing Sheridan and feeling the slosh of brews in the stomach, sucking down a Camel to exacerbate and exorcise the hunger, and the *finally* feeling it all brings. Where would a writer focus? There's no story, no starting point. What is the tone? Orgasmic? Do they teach that at J school? Anyways, it'd have to be one of those *New Yorker* think pieces that stretches on toward infinity, covering every angle, to the point where the "continued on" notice is followed by a made up number followed by some letters, nobody's going that deep, nobody's following that break. Though I currently write for a more everyman rag, a tad humbler in scope, leaner and more frugal with payments to its freelancers, I keep on, after it, dodge the six lanes of what is, by this hour, at least 50-percent half-drunk traffic, and continue toward the neon light promising flattop sizzle and smoke and magic, and push forth with my own brand of paperwork.

4. BUFFALO (5-2)

"'The Boys are Back in Town,' you 'member that one?" Uncle Ike asks, as if I was born and cognizant at a time when the track wasn't played on classic rock radio, as though I might remember when it dropped, me and my buds ripping bongs on a Friday night basement couch, listening to the Cars, or whoever does that song.

Uncle Ike is in town, inexplicably, unannounced, and the only reason, decent or otherwise, that I find myself in Caputi's on a weekday afternoon, shooting pool and bitching about the jukebox. Our second pitcher of beer is on a nearby table and there are some guys sizing us up the way pool hall guys do, all shoulders and chin, looking like they want to call next and wondering what's the deal with the chubby-ish dude in the Bills cap and the Popeye-armed Mustache he's taking to school.

"These assholes put this on?"

It's a rhetorical question, not directed at me, more at the head-shaking state of society, kids today, of everything wrong, of all the bullshit, and leveled by Ike without so much as lifting his gaze in the directions of the Caputi's afternoon regulars. They're the classic sort to hang in a shitty sports bar, of indeterminate age, out-of-work construction workers or disability-leave ranch house inheritors. Playing overhead is something bad, pop-ish and bass-y and delivered poorly by the neon-lit contraption in the corner my father's brother keeps calling 'the juke,' but pronouncing it with emphasis, *jewwwwk*, the source of so much fist-making consternation on his part. It's not my easy way with the bar games, nor the surprising drubbing I can dish out, but there's little doubt he's now in a hurry to get one back, split the series, and return to the bar even, or even enough, his testicular fortitude evident, so some serious, seated drinking can commence.

"What's wrong with the fucking *Allman Brothers*?" he asks, and immediately scratches the cue ball, maybe intentionally, maybe to spite the juke and the jerks with their quarters and Tonawanda lives. Or maybe to prove his doneness with the game, and the surrounding bullshit.

"Bullshit," he keeps saying, everything covered in it somehow, the word coming from a place down near his lower intestines and arriving with a tiny spritz of venomous spittle. To someone that didn't know him, these assholes perhaps—and I myself have come to see them as assholes now, or half-see them, I avoid direct glances, just get a feel for presence and degrees of threat my uncle is wordlessly projecting—he might seem to puff out his chest as he turns back toward his stool, the bar, and the cardboard coaster he's already told me he's stealing 10 of because they have the Bills schedule printed on them, but that is merely his stature, that of a man who would be standing in the shadows behind a very bad man in a sit-down type of scene in every bar in every gangster flick.

It's an easy shadow to ride in, and it usually takes place out west, cruising sunny Oakland streets, him showing me the 'hood and the burrito joints, all of which he deems infinitely more appropriate than anything found in San Francisco, a place whose tech and yuppie bent is generally perceived as either *not-manly* or homosexually *button-down*. So instead we wander through Fruitvale, and by the Hell's Angels headquarters. Down International Boulevard, and through potholed griminess. By his favorite bookstores, in and out of his favorite bars. By old places he used to live, upon first relocating, traversing the topography of a transplanted, fleeing Buffalonian. The DNA of a hulking 'Ski, popping his Marlboro Red against the cracked window of a black, borrowed SUV, something vaguely blue-collar and my-town proud about the whole picture. Here though, in Caputi's, with schoolmates of either of ours bound to walk through the front door at any moment, or out of the bathroom with a noseful, everything seems skewed. Like two too many on a weeknight, like when you get up for your stop too early and the bus is still going and you've misjudged the inertia and need another couple steps for balance. His being is out of context, the West Coast so many years away it makes his current shirt seem too small, and there's at once a chip back on his shoulder, and again something to prove, something from backseats, crowded lunchrooms, unattended funerals—an agitating thing to get away from.

I follow him back to our seats and the bartender and her tank top—white, tip-encouraging, flirt-yielding to the manlier among us. I try, mostly, not to look.

"What are we doing here?" Ike asks.

"Drinking, pissing, checking that broad's tits, and going back to Grandma's," I say, and take what I hope appears a man-sized swig of Molson in advance of a booming belch that won't come, looking like I'm yawning instead.

"But fuck, what are *you* doing here?"

Sometime after Super Bowl 25, and "wide right," and the subsequent death of my father; after the endless replays of Norwood's missed game-winner had begun to dissipate, and the following loss and loss and loss, the sadness of four straight Super Bowl let-downs settled over Buffalo like dust from a test bomb. And not the atom kind, with invisible radiation and silent cancer, but rather with visible grime and debris of a more quotidian sort, where you go to clean the window, spray and rub, only to realize the dirt is on the *outside*. After Ike had split for the farthest golden shores of California and my brother had taken his own game a few states over for college and half-assed Manifest Destiny-ing, before the fateful 500-mile ride for little Teddy, with caretakers and cat, to the skyscrapered tip of "Chicago" that really turned out to be anywheresville suburbia, as 'Skis, we collectively decided that this wasn't the place for us. Not anymore. As it goes with these things, though, it went unspoken, and all those things left unsaid—here, now, with the

28

Bills logos over the walls and the Sabres neon beer lights around us, the pitchers stoking something besides the need for more beer — seem to sprout up between even the most mundane conversational cracks like weeds.

"I'm gonna write it all down," I tell him, "get that shit published, make a fuck ton of money, take a shot, fuck that chick in the bathroom, beat your ass in another game of pool, go chow Helka's beef, and then have one more beer. Winner, winner, chicken wing dinner."

"Some old Fleetwood. That'd be right about now." Ike swallows deep and gazes far away, taking a cocktail napkin off the bar to ball with his fist, taking another deep pull.

There's almost no warning for what happens next, and certainly no reason. The thing I notice first, the thing I'll remember later, like squealing brakes before an accident, is the noise. It's not broken glass or any kind of crash, but a *thwuuump* that signifies a breath's quick, unexpected departure from the body, the solid echo of an Adam's Apple, and the crumbling of a tall fellow I barely had a look at till now, and still it's just a corner-of-the-eye glimpse. I have to remind myself to swallow the mouthful of beer, because something's happened.

I'd never seen a throat punch before. I still haven't, such is the speed and whiplash-like *whatthefuck*-ery with which it transpired. Ike is standing by the time our non-friend hits the floor, both his fists clenched, lower jaw jutting just a bit. A sparkle of spittle on his mustache, his face backlit in rigid profile, his back muscles hardened and hunched up and forward, as if they themselves are saying *lemme at him*, and something off in his eye, "Street Fighting Man" or some such business should clearly be starting on the juke, and at an aggressive volume.

"We're leaving, we're leaving," I say, my hands on Ike, blood-flowing, pulsing, leaning, testosterone-popped toward aggressive mediation, leaving half a beer, not wanting to ruin a potentially nice dinner, playing it cool, thinking, *it's alright, just don't let him kill this guy.*

"He'll close his tab," Ike says, stoically, calmly nodding his head toward the dude on the floor clutching at his windpipe to delineate exactly who will be closing out, finishing his own beer in a single gulp and placing the pint glass squarely on the bartop.

"We're going, we're going..." I say again, this time with my arms up, surrendering, the bartender confused and O-faced making her way down toward the quick and subtle commotion, not sure what's going on but frightened anyway, and then I'm on Ike's chest and back, pushing him toward the door, masculating or emasculating, whichever it is, the blood in my face pulsing, the confusion settling into acceptance, time seeming urgent, my pushes segueing into back-slaps, by now realizing it's more of a hush falling over the place than a melee and we're probably, almost definitely, not going to jail, if we can just get out of here, back into the fall air and over toward Grandma's.

"Ike, shit. Fuck."

"What?"

"You just throat-punched that guy."

"What? You wanted to stick around?"

"Well, I was gonna let you win a game of pool." I light a cigarette, forearming my forehead and glancing over my shoulder at the door, wondering where his buddies are, if they are coming, hurrying a bit, pushing Ike square in the back and hastening my steps, thinking we should have pre-called Grandma for a ride.

"You've already lost."

"Yeah?"

"Yeah. Serious." He pulls a bottle of Labatt's from his hoodie gut pocket, cracking the top with his lighter, swilling deep, wiping his 'stache with a trigger-shaped, sausage index finger permanently stained with carburetor grease, or something more nefarious.

I take the bottle and sip some myself as we jaywalk across Sheridan. He doesn't look back, lumbering slow, early evening settling over the city and imaginative wafts of Grandma's roast beef easing our collective bad Buffalo blood, calling us home.

"How's that, Uncle?" I hand him back the bottle, wondering how a man could hate a song so, as he holds out his palm and cups and uncups his index finger to ask for one of my Camels.

"You were born here."

5. CHICAGO (2-1)

I've been considering asking Dustin to move in with me.

I don't want to freak him out, naturally, but it is nearing the beginning of Week Four, which means we've already shared close to three weeks of busted-hymen friendship and Bills camaraderie and hard beer drinking and laughter—a completely ceaseless wandering between uproarious bellows and exhausted giggles. Always, the two of us, with the dropping to the knees, the hair-pulling on third downs, the signs of the cross and the half-sprints across the bar with arms straight in the air and fists at the end of said arms, such little jogs always ending in rough hugs and hearty open-palmed pats on the back, and laughs.

It's just good economics: between his need to do a shot of Powers after every touchdown *and* extra point—"we just scored *again*"—and the Bills' surprisingly potent offense—Fred Jackson leading the league in touchdowns, catching the ball with one hand sometimes, seemingly for our sheer delight, before turning upfield with great malice, and for us to be able to turn to each other, hands on heads in disbelief, wide-eyed, and with exhilaration say, "Jesus, Freddie. Ya did it, you bastard. Jesus!"—our tabs are running rather high. There's also the subtly building chance that our back pats are now a bit too jocular even for dickheaded sports bar company. Not to mention his maybe overwrought frustration move of gripping the padded barstool with both mitts, lifting the seat, which he never thinks about using for intended sitting purpose after kickoff, and smashing the legs against the floor with Kruschev-like malevolence. This generally precedes a diatribe about what's wrong with the front office, with quarterback Fitzgerald, usually with both arms cocked at 90-degree angles and a look on his scrunched up face like his mother just told him he was adopted, and like he's thinking about calling somebody right now, to clear this whole gridiron matter up.

I've practiced the argument in my head a number of times, with only positive results:

I'll take care of the cleaning, plus I got a pretty decent stereo. Gonna pick up some speaker stands one of these days, even. I make pretty nice tacos, too, can go ground beef in what I call Tedcos, har-har, or I get the chorizo from the Mexican grocery and cook it nice and crispy and then drain it and throw some white onion and serranos or jalapenos in there and crisp it a bit more, and let the peppers get toasty, and if I do say so myself I got the queso-melting on a warm tortilla method down solid. And then we can get the NFL package on the dish and we don't ever have to get dressed on Sundays, just chill in our lion pants – oh, yeah, that's a bit weird, I call my pajama pants 'lion pants' because their for lyin' around, HAHA! – yeah, so we can not get dressed and then I'll warm up the meat at halftime if it's already made and we can have like a taco bar, or I could make you nachos in the broiler with some fresh tomato and maybe sour cream while you call out what's going on around the league in your loud voice and I'll hear you in the kitchen and I'll say something like 'Shit, really?' or 'Awww, fuck!' And then we can talk about the Super Bowl years and I'll bring you a fresh beer without you having to ask, and we'll click bottles and you'll say thanks and then we'll both sit back...

But the real convincer, the closer, is the money we'd save on beers.

There's that certain time around your mid-twenties, or later, if you're me, where you realize drinking at bars makes almost no sense. And you do it anyway, but start to acknowledge, then think, and then know, that yes, absolutely, by comparison and anybody's math, drinking at home is pretty much free. So we can accept this, together, this newfound friend and I, and we won't need anybody else.

I'll lay it all out for him: how we'll watch my VHS recording of the Comeback Game—our finest moment, but the one only we can grasp, understand, like a wedding video you're trying to show second cousins once removed—on Friday nights after ordering pizza.

I can see it, how I'll fiddle with the tracking knob and joke about modern technology. I could get some baked wings going here and there, and always have a fridge full of heady after-work brews. Always have Frank's Red Hot on hand, and maple syrup too—the sauce recipe always just an ask away for him. I know a pretty legit dealer but I'll save that as something to mention later, as a bit of a housewarming, welcome-to-our-life present.

Welcome to our new life, old friend.

I see myself Price Is Right-sweeping an open palm across the living room as he walks in with a big duffel and bigger smile, an *I can't believe we're doing this* twinkle about his eyes. He'll look down at the coffee table next and get a Christmas-day-like surprise upon his brow and exclaim, "We can smoke in here!?"

As is the way with adult dealings, Smoke himself has happened to be around my life less and less, by degrees. Suddenly weekend nights kicking back and forth on the smelly couches, when we used to make fun of each other's football teams and argue about which bar to go to once the beers are gone, are far more often solo affairs. I mix up my seat each time back from the fridge, to keep it interesting, like there's a dialogue between selves, the cat looking at me like I'm a dick each time. *Go to bed already, dude,* he's always saying, *I'll cover your feet with my fat stomach,* and I smile back, that drunk and alone smile all true drunks have, even when sad, for themselves, never to show anyone, signifying complete and resigned victory over the world.

Saturday afternoons used to feature a hodgepodge drinking collective, Friday's leftover bottles of beer plus some from my own stash and those of whomever else stumbled by, but these days it seems like everybody has heard of my looming, possible, departure for Buffalo, and despite the plane tickets not yet purchased, the assignment not yet assigned, and with a still universal, at-large acceptance that I'm rather happy and will continue to go on living, trying, nobody's in much hurry to hang out or consider me part of their weekend playbook. Since I'm moving but not, like, *moving*, there exists no proper finality.

Does Ted have cancer?

No.

OK, we can hang out next month.

There also exists, wafting, among certain near-30-somethings around me, a new notion resembling white flight, a long-accepted abhorrence of suburbia that seems to be washing away in subtle waves that echo and sound like *baby* and *house* but feel, at times, like giving up. This rings truest every time I make it to the kitchen for another Sierra Nevada and have to pin a "Save the Date" to the refrigerator with my left hand as I use the bottle opener magnet with my right, before replacing it over some one-time drinking buddy's photoshopped mug, pinning him there with a reminder of another compromised weekend six-to-eight months from now. There's always one more, they arrive near every other week, and I wonder how so many people have so much time to take so many professional pictures.

I wonder also how my own life might fare under such lensed scrutiny. Since Smoke's newfound distance I've taken to lowering the heat as an excuse to don a blanket as both superhero cape and warming device, trotting between emails, pitches, and kitchen coffee-making sessions like Don Quixote of the North Side. Still, at the very least, I'm not moving to Mt. Prospect Heights View, I tell myself. No Skokieeee for me. I don't even know where Downers Grove is. I actually keep coming back toward Pilsen, myself, as an idea, as an embodiment of adulthood of a different kind, my own spiteful, fist-shaking sort.

But here, in Bucktown, I have the spot already. Half-have, actually, but half is close. The neighborhood is fine enough, very decent corn-tortilla tacos nearby, even late at night, and in easy striking distance to a full-fledged professionalistic adulthood, too. Once the book hits, I won't have far to go to the top, but since I'm more keen on Buffalo and bottoms these days, and with the growing, cutting fall wind, what's the point of boxing all this shit up? Worrying about scrounging extra funds for a new security deposit is more a pursuit for one's early-20s.

A new roommate is only a simple, persuasive conversation away. I can grease the wheels if I make the habanero cream sauce, but it has to be the right meatstuff to combine it with, so, still, there's planning to do. There's also the matter of getting him over to the pad without being too weird or come-on-ish. We may also need to get some pleasantries, logistics, and niceties covered: discuss what each of us does for a living, or what either of us *wants* to do, or discuss anything, really, not pertaining to Jim Kelly, Duff's, or the best place for a late drink in Allentown—a neighborhood in a city where neither of us have lived for over 10 years. And there's the beaten-back fact that someone with a new title and a weighty presence in my life, with an opinion on where my hat hangs and what kind of hat I should wear and how much the brim should be bent, may not be wholly happy with this decision.

Then again, here are two people who have maybe found what they're looking for. Here we have it, like a scene from Disney, like a climax with its own string section score, like the replays of the kicker and holder when everything goes right and they jump-embrace in best-friendship, bursting public male caresses, and there's no need for death or entire family displacement from the region. Mates separated at birth, fatefully realigned, what has been in the stars since rubbing faces on their respective mother's vulvas and being spit into the snow-swirled gray-itude of Bills fandom. Inexplicable warm togetherness in the sad, windy isolation of Chicago, and for the first time in a while, despite the blows, the indifference, the concrete anonymity of my town, the sad slip into everyman late-20s potential-squandering doesn't seem so bleak.

36

6. MIGHTY TACO
1762 Sheridan Dr.
Buffalo NY, 14223

The way to walk through a drive-thru window is without hesitation. No apologies, shrugs, laughs, or explanations. As if it's the most natural thing in the world. In fact, adopting an air of annoyance can be a boon. Like dealing with cops: aloofness, hurry, chippiness, a checking-of-the-wrist-watch-and-clearing-the-throat and *ahem* are talismans of a straight citizen doing nothing wrong, with nothing to hide. It helps demand respect.

I don't have time for all this.

-

I'll take 3 beef and cheese burritos.

-

I've got plenty of important things to do.

-

And a side of nachos.

-

Please, I need to get back to work.
Anything else?
Make it 4.
That's it?
I can't be bothered with this now, just 5 burritos, hot, no sour cream.

The best bet is to have Grandma's twenty—so crisp and sharp-cornered, fresh from the mint, it seems, pulled from one of those little white envelopes that only contain cash, blow, or diamonds— already in hand. No time for fumbling, like catching the bartender's eye with seriousness of intent, so that the drive-thru girl, always so lovely—is it the Mighty Taco hat, or her holding, in that plastic bag, the key to everything?—watching you through the camera will have no doubts, no hesitations, no need to call a manager or remind of their "liability" policy or some such legal mumbo jumbo in relation to being a pedestrian in a drive-thru.

I got the twenty, fresh from Grandma's purse, and I intend to spend it all…

The fat quotient in the beef here has long been a matter of spirited, sometimes acrimonious, debate. Johnny claims he once replicated the consistency with a 70-30 beef fat ratio. Ike states you have to light a candle, drink six Molsons, and play the Comeback Game with full volume, uninterrupted, for the last hour of defrosting – also, you have to use 70-30 ground beef. A bartender at a dimly-lit joint on Elmwood, after pouring a Baker's, lighting my smoke, and glancing around to make sure nobody was listening, told me in hushed tones you can't buy it, because the cow's used are actually weaned on *ground beef*. As to the fat content, he couldn't, or wouldn't, say for sure, but he ventured a guess at 70-30. Mom brought some back to Chicagoland last Christmas, and before me, to my consternation, audibly defamed and scourged every bite, claiming herself unimpressed, spouting nonsense such as "no big deal" and "it's just a taco," and proceeded to violently wolf two reheated behemoths before her son stepped in, swiping the last mishandled meat ship that needed tender caresses, proper love, while she pretended not to be hurt. It wasn't until a bite was threatened that she acquiesced, offering meekly, "Wait a second…"

What to make of it, for someone engorged on *al pastor* and *chilaquiles* and *cecina* and the double-corn-cilantro-onion fair of every-corner Chicago? What of the lacking authenticity and the chain-like feel, the neon lights and silly burrito names, and the complete absence of Mexican culture throughout its native city? What to tell someone that claims, fairly, that it is neither burrito nor taco? Or the friend that talks about how *processed* it is, like the P-word is the C-word of foodstuffs, as if a verb that loosely means *handled or managed* is the equivalent of a genocide, calorically-speaking? And what of the hall monitor who thinks about, for your sake and *for the love of God Almighty, your Cholesterol?*

What to do is punch that person directly in the throat, the Adam's Apple if possible, take the *Buffito* out of their ungracious, pampered hands, slick the sour cream off with a spoon or the inside of your pinky, and enjoy life without further comment.

This would be the place to write about, the place by which to sell an uncertain editor — an editor with eyebrow scrunches, always pushing glasses back up on nose to look down, a boss not wanting to pay for a vision quest of validation, full of disregard of hopeful note-jotting — on the special otherness of Buffalo's eating. This would be the place to journalistically investigate, to probe every single franchise location: to rank, in slideshow form for optimum hits, the 10 best counter servers, the 12 best hangover cures on the menu, the cleanest bathrooms for number two purposes, the best bathrooms for hungover number two purposes, the best drive-thru to walk through after five hours of no-nonsense Canadian beer drinking at Caputi's.

Such are the flights of poetic reverie, of fanciful keyboard-banging, once back at Grandma's. A Molson sweating on the coffee table wood, *Cheers* laugh-tracking low in the background hardly noticed. Grandma sitting in her chair, wondering what I'm looking at, why I'm scribbling lunatic scribbles, what the deal is with the soft moans and throaty *mmm*-ing purrs that escape after every bite, not getting at all why I stop between burritos one and two to remove my corduroys. I continue on in my boxers, greasing up the pen and pad occasionally, Grandma herself enjoying a little chicken fajita that I've not been quite dickhead enough to forget, pausing during canned laughter of the TV to ask, or more so to marvel, with head shaking, "You *enjoy* your Mighty Taco." And she says it, mouth open, while chewing.

Helka denture smacks matter little, though, what with the

Swiss-ish American-like cheese happily gooping and swirling like warm taffy over and around the meat, and the hot sauce like magically spiced tomato paste, surprising when it pops up and asserts its tang, and the beef granules running into one another, bonding, becoming chummy—*hey how ya doing? Nice we're gonna be together for a bit, eh?*—sliding along on their own grease, like horny speed daters, coming together, breaking apart, all heat and tension and moistness. It's one of the few meals where I think on my gut more than my own happiness, the organ making assertive noises now, smiling, I imagine, as welcoming as a gracious host at a holiday party throwing back the front door—*just throw your jacket on the bed in that room, what can I get you? Sure, sure, ha, ha, the more the merrier*—not thinking about tomorrow.

It would take maybe 18 burritos to rupture a normal, adult human stomach. Somehow I've always known the answer, this answer, to the Last Meal question, and have always been waiting for someone to ask.

7. BUFFALO (5-3)

"What the fuck happened with Ike?" Johnny asks, cracking a Genessee Cream Ale and settling back into Grandma's knockoff Lazy Boy, easing off his boots just before kickoff and taking a contented swill.

"Somebody said something about Super Bowl 25, I think." I'm wearing my lion pants, nursing beer number two and a judging glare from Grandma that seems to clear its own throat and give an *at least put some pants on, you gonna drink all that beer.*

"Aww, shit..." The understanding is instant, complete, the pitcher getting the signal he wanted, the only further explanation needed of a different sort. "And he didn't *kill* the fucker?"

"Lucky I was there. And lucky for that fucker I know how to handle *our* fucker."

It's Week Nine, and the inevitable sour turn has begun. Like buying avocados, the promise on market day great—guacamole with onions and lime juice, some diced jalapenos, enough for Sunday game day nachos and maybe a turkey-guac sandwich with the leftovers for Monday lunch—but they're soft now, mushy, unappetizing, regrettable. Too dark, in two days, and of course you can't eat them, but they were expensive, so you crack one open to be sure and can't even handle it without the impression of a thumb immediately appearing on the surface. You feel physically strong, crushing life without even trying, but spiritually drained. Just like that, in less than two quarters of a nationally-televised embarrassment, at the hands of the Jets, no less.

As I go for my third beer Grandma is fiddling with the thermostat for the second time since he arrived, asking Johnny if he's warm enough in his thin t-shirt (t-shirts are inherently "thin" to Grandma: they could be made of burlap, but if the cut exposes the forearm at all, it's not getting the job done in three out of four Buffalo seasons). I pass him and say, "Johnny, you warm enough, we can get that heat up to 90," with a faux-concerned pat on the thigh and a thought that this isn't so bad. I could move in for good, take over the extra bedroom, get Johnny a cot in the living room so he doesn't need to stay at his former bass player's house. Grandma can scratch each of our backs, in turn, not at the same time, mind you, but tasteful-like. Maybe it's the coming buzz, the noon-ish variety that precedes a pizza and a nap, and later Round Two at Caputi's, for the night game, that second drunk of the day like a bonus, like a smile from God and a reminder to waste no time, no days, none of Grandma's dough that could be yielded on the sporty Sunday night barmaid who's always ready to let me buy her a shot of Jameson while pretending not to notice her cleavage. I tell my neck muscles they can't retract, my head's not that heavy, they're not that nice, don't look, not yet, just wait till she turns. And who needs playoff tension anyhow?

Johnny doesn't care because it's almost time for the halftime order, that's why he's really here. "Can you believe the fucking contract this fucking guy gets?" he says, knocking his head back and shaking the can in my general direction with a nod, eyebrow-up eye contact, the universal plea for another.

"The language, Johnny!" Grandma shouts. "Keep that up and I'll smack that face." When her blood pressure spikes you can almost hear the beeps on that machine, upping the tempo, like a jazz drummer, Helka always looking to swing.

Johnny leans forward and sticks his jaw out, purses his lower lip, a perfect invite for a devastating uppercut.

"Grandma, punch that fucking face of his, please. Look at that thing. That jaw."

"The face only a mother could love," Grandma says, on her game after her second cup of really bad coffee, reveling in a Bills loss in her own way. Like me, unable to accept success, to know what to do with what was a decent record and modicum of midseason respectability. Being in the race is exhausting: our family motto.

"A grandmother, too," Johnny says, "if she could see."

I give Johnny a fist bump for this one and hand him a beer, cracking my own, letting some spray jizz up and money shot a bit on my new Fred Jackson tee. Grandma guffaws, and Grandma guffaws in a nightgown are not her finest hour, not the time for the portrait artist or sculpture guy, not with that look on her face, the hurt *what happened to you* face, like once a week when you tell her you're *not fucking going to church.*

"If Grandpa could hear you bums talk like this…"

"That dead bastard? Please." I get an air high-five from Johnny from the next seat over. The Bills respond themselves with a three-and-out, a fluttery too-much-air fly pattern on third-and-five falling benignly among some bench players and sideline-randoms. I always wonder who those guys are, not the black guys in street clothes that look tough and hungry and just two weeks away from gladiatorial work, and not the polacks holding the game balls, but the ones in suits, standing around. Whatever those guys do, I should have majored in *that.*

The mention of the original Johnny, or "O.G. Johnny" as we've taken to calling him, the bit of original gangster-ness both hilarious and apt, classically out-of-place but deserved, hangs over the room, as it does even without a mention. His picture sits in a little frame on the table between Johnny and I, a black and white number from his Army days, him wearing those sharp whites, bell-bottoms for some reason even though I thought that was only the chaps in the Navy that sported such. He's at a bar, gazing wistfully, smoking a cigarette in the fashion of people that could once smoke with ease and normalcy, without the guilty stare of virgin air, without looking like ill-willed degenerates or motherless child-murderers. Freely, with enviable ignorance. Old days liberation from all this laboratory and headlines-about-health tyranny. Content, in control, his jaw level, like men used to look when wars were to be won, and women to be courted. Despite being in some Panamanian jungle hellhole, feasted on by four mosquitoes at that very moment, probably not even good tacos nearby, while the unknown photog pulls a candid on ol' 'Ski getting charmingly drunk, like I always picture myself between beers four and five at Caputi's, before him and his buddies retire and hope for a night free of sirens and scorpions.

Could he have sensed his destiny then, deep in the trees, grappling Nazism and the like? Did he see it, gazing out on a sunset over the canal, or a single palm tree, whatever: marrying the night-gowned guffaw queen of North Buffalo, and producing the likes of Ike, with his many notches on the throat-punch gun, and Ike's brother, who in turn yielded two perpetual eating contest runners-up currently getting aimlessly Bills drunk on a Sunday afternoon in a house he built with bare hands (so I was led to believe), unshaven, unshowered, and in at least one of their cases, not truly panted? Would he have wanted to argue with life and what she held, her hands cupping all of that, a smorgasbord platter of undeserved disappointment, offered with grace and a smile? If he could see it, this now, splayed all out in drunken foresight in that Central American watering hole, what would he say?

Can't that kinda fat one get dressed? And aren't they worried they're going to run out of beer?

At least he got the Super Bowl years. At least we all got the Super Bowl years. Among the teeming, toiling lot of pre-cancer patients every cognizant human counts themselves a part, all of us just waiting for the *Take that trip, dammit* from the wizened old doctor, among this particular gathering—the current living room, down the street at Caputi's, all of Tonawanda, most of-a-certain-age Buffalonians— there is the attitude of *I took that fucking trip. Now, if you please, Doc, can you cure this motherfucker so I can wait around for another?*

The halftime order comes with three minutes left in the third quarter, such is the menu debate and willful delaying of gratification. "Another one. Let's have one more then call." And while the call is being made Fitz is on his backside watching a no-name linebacker run, actually trot, back the easiest pick-six of an unheralded career. Dan Dierdorf gasps in disgust, the replay a thing of horror on every TV set in the city, Grandma guffaws *of course*, while disappointment echoes about the empty streets. Fitz has a rare talent for instant failure. It's like a "hot read," but something Dustin has labeled instead a "not read," and he has just had one, his bearded jaw on his chest before the reverse touchdown is even inside the 20-yard line, a man we've never heard of already dancing, his grandfather up in heaven gazing down with a knowing half-smile, the way they do in movie denouements, the revelation of an unspoken delineation between those meant to win, and those meant for pepperoni contemplation. There's the inevitable close-up, and I realize I've recently gained an unseemly familiarity with the Fitz chin strap, or, more precisely, with the inside of it—the way it looks, dangling, unsnapped in disgusted resignation, when the merciless cameraman zooms hard for a close-1 shot after a pick, to get the *Uh-hhh* disappointed face. It's like constipation and failure to perform at once. The more things change, the more bad things happen, or however that saying goes.

Eventually, pizza helps. Extra sauce, jalapenos on the side. Rivulets of grease run down the mozzarella like there are great Roman aqueducts leading toward our mouths. Hydrating, nourishing, maintaining harmony. Johnny's not finishing bites, just starting the next one. He got himself a plate but has either forgotten it or abandoned such an idea as so much window-dressing. He's now just leaning forward to pull back a triangle, getting his fingers under the body, lifting it high, dangling the falling front cheese—always there, so reluctant to pull away from his friends, his brothers in the middle pie lines—above his mouth.

"So seductive, John boy. So sexy."

He has no napkin, either. Very no frills, very bare bones, taking only what's necessary for survival, he would have done well in the Donner Party. Of course, he's not beating me to the death gut punch, and he's most certainly not beating me in the slice-counting category, either. With an eight slice large pie, one piece is reserved for Grandma—it's our Sunday act of charity, I don't even scalp a slice of pepperoni from her piece. And that leaves the better man to topple four toothsome, grease-happy slices.

"How's your bride-to-be?" Johnny asks.

"Whaddya mean, I just met him."

"Huh." Johnny knows he's got me, distracting, already raising another slice, severing the stretchy cheese bit with left-hand malice.

"Oh. Wait. Who?" And I'm blushing, lost, sheepish in my inability to read a defense and getting one-upped, out-classed, intercepted.

"Could I have another slice?" Grandma asks meekly, waiting for a TV commercial to turn towards us, blinking through cataracts and empty hope.

"Not if you want to see tomorrow."

She shuffles off toward the bathroom with an air of hurt, defeated *aw shucks* fist-swinging, thinking she should have stayed at church and appearing as though she might stop to kick at some dirt like a down-on-his-luck Okie.

"What's her problem? *Another slice? Seriously?"*

"She's been a real bastard of late."

"Yeah, since about the time she turned 60."

I lean forward and snag a forgotten crust off of Grandma's otherwise clean plate, stick it in my mouth like a cigar, pretend to light up. That gets a "Nice!" from Johnny and a vehement air hand slap exchanged from across the room by us two bloated sacks of Buffalo pride reclining in struggling Lazy Boy-like fluffs. We eventually sit back and fold our hands across our pained bellies and I reach over to O.G. Johnny's picture frame—so stoic, so Clark Gable, and how does he keep his mustache so prim in the goddamn Tropics?—and turn it toward the wall, facing away from the floundering football team currently going for it on fourth down because there's no point in punting when it's 28-10 this late in the fourth.

8. CHICAGO (0-0)

Weeks before the season—a now-unthinkable realm before Dustin and understanding and light and belonging, and, inevitably, reality and terrible marauding Bills-season darkness, with the summer days beginning to grow shorter, overnight almost, exclamation pointing the coming end with that weird red apocalyptic glow that seems to highlight what summer evenings used to mean way back when: baseball, ice cream, sweaty backseat gropery, illicit beers out of trunks in parking lots and new friendships instantly formed with whomever could procure said beers, freedom, not having to make decisions, decisions like this—there is a decision to be made.

Freshly-shaven and pulling myself away from the computer, from the checking of email and the occasional stop-and-gaze at cartoon Kerouac, always self-consciously, as if there was a camera on my brooding contemplation, a portrait of the artist as a young wanker, something like that, I am to meet the fiancé to look at an apartment. Or condo, as she called it on the phone, but I never knew the difference, it being one of those things that if you wait too long into childhood to ask, you never can. Like how I was with the whole stocks-versus-bonds thing. The clitoris, the idea of it, another example. I must have been sick the day we covered that mythical spectrum in freshman year Health class. Probably at home masturbating, somewhat ironically.

My only understanding is that there is a building, one that can be lived in for more than a few nights, for a certain amount of agreed upon money per month, to be seen to. Questions are to be asked, water pressure to be checked, bare knuckles rapped against walls, faces scrunched at the inherent oddities all living quarters have.

"Why is there a lazy susan *there?*"

"What's a lazy susan? And what is she *supposed* to be doing? Maybe she's not lacking purpose, but direction. And with this economic climate it's hard right now."

That kind of thing. I am to meet the fiancé at some random Wicker Park corner at a time that I have deemed as far too early, thus relegating myself, prematurely, to be in the middle of a fight when I show up 15 minutes late, smoking a cigarette, fresh coffee in hand, feeling fine aside from the massive inconvenience of being out of the apartment. On a weekend, no less, when work is going well, writing is grooving, synonyms are plucking themselves out of the air, metaphors dropping like, I don't know, raindrops or something. With clauses endless, editors responding, even positively—if I read between the lines a bit, and do I ever—time away from the computer feels like a short-change to artistic progress, to advancing cultural insight, to further Proust-like flights, to oeuvre-making, to a budding bildungsroman, to society and her understanding of herself as a whole.

"Just ask questions, ok?" Lindsay, aka Fiancé, aka X, says, not happy, very much not getting a wet clitoris over my kiss on the cheek, despite my fresh-shaven, professional-type chin.

"Any particular topic?" Me, spirited, worried, but floating, as 1,500 words quickly followed by a paycheck can do like nothing else this side of chicken wings and a win. This is still the offseason, of course, so societal servitude in the form of a think piece on the merits of traveling to and eating and getting diarrhea in New Orleans, and a subsequent rewarding piece of paper, one to take to the bank, feels like the tops.

"This is our future, take it seriously. Fuck."

"Ok, X. Studs Turkel mode is fucking on."

Somewhere after dropping about 10 articles-worth of salary on a 4mm-wide metal circle, a tiny sphere I was certain she'd lose, not because she was that type, just because it'd be hilarious to lose something so expensive, I started referring to Lindsay as my ex-girlfriend, or simply 'X'. She was no longer my girlfriend, and for that I was sad.

"But these things happen," as I would tell the bartender, or Smoke, or whoever was around, with a straight face, before busting up with the punchline, and maybe a "zing!"

Our landlord, or "realtor," as she calls herself, is an Asian woman with impossible cheekbones. All business and all business suit, moving with purpose, pride, the immaculate posture of an MBA-mannequin, Feminist model. She's the clear-eyed kind that instantly makes you feel her lesser, like you should be hitting your browser's back button and searching for a porn actress more in line with your social standing. Even right after you shake her hand and realize you forgot to tuck in your shirt, and you're suddenly very conscious of how you're standing. I'd like to know where she lives, how big her bathtub is, where she went to school, what her Christmases are like—fluffy snow in Vermont, or the beach?—if she knows where to get good Thai. The inquisitiveness settles in, real and forced.

"Does Piece deliver this far?"

"Well, I, uh… Peace?"

"No matter, I know the driver. Well, *drivers*, I'll work something out." I'm on my knees, head under the kitchen sink, inspecting, fingering, making noise, putzing around as much as possible without giving myself a hangnail—hangnails being the very reason to avoid such bending and squatting and the sticking of heads under sinks.

"What is this pipe? PPC?" I affect a plumber's crack even, quite manly.

"PVC?" the realtor asks, confused.

"Ehh," I groan, incredulous, half-disappointed.

It's one of those days you see in the first act of movies, a movie your mom likes, with a couple floating through an empty hardwood floor-ed, high-ceilinged, turn-of-the-century apartment that's all class and snoot and elegance. With the woman in some kind of dress, practically floating between rooms, not comprehending why she has it so good, and the man in his suit but without a tie, some five-o'clock shadow going to show the viewer it's his day off, or Saturday, eyes googly on his woman, not caring about the pad he's about to throw one million down on, intent only on making her happy. She hasn't even realized it yet, but, yes, pull that blind back, and huzzah!

"Oh, Harold, it has a view of the park!"

"Not to mention a great school district." He's outdoing himself, probably even speaking in an affected British accent.

"Oh, but, can we afford it!?" She has both hands over her heart, her clitoris is doing a thing, some kind of thing, I think.

"Our love can afford all things." He might even get down on his knees for this one, have something to give her, something that was his Mamie's, a watch, or a pendant, whatever a pendant is, from the old country, some such token of his undying and boundless and endless enamorment. He uses those words, too, "undying," and he describes how said Mamie had to hide something from the malevolent Third Reich inside her lady parts, and how it can unify them in an "endless" fashion.

"Can you hear the neighbors doing it?" I ask, with scrunched-up eyebrows and my fingers tapping my mouth in a moment of reposed thoughtfulness.

Of course the realtor in the movie, the dear old spinster with her binder, was holding something back, and by the end of Act Two the man and woman hate each other, or have come to realize a gruesome double-homicide was committed in the guest bedroom and the smudge in the Mr. Coffee is red-hued and that's why they can't sleep. Or there's undisclosed ovarian failure and the woman has nightmares about her entrails and a never-born demon baby, with a grin, playing gaily amongst her glistening, slithery fallopian tubes in the dining room. Or her uterus is fine, normal, fertile, it's just that he's a terminal case. Or he starts banging his secretary because she's always wearing those business suit dresses and the librarian glasses and she's more exotic and understands his passion for Chablis and doggy-style.

X is giving me a funny look and I stroke my clean chin as an act of solidarity, showing I'm doing my part, playing the role—nurturer, provider, protector, neighborhood-watcher.

"There many violent sexual assaults in this neighborhood?" I ask.

This one throws her, I bet she's never heard it, never before seen a man so primed for grizzled, shielding masculinity. I might as well go right now to gather some wood and start making a fire, shield the woman folk from sabre-tooths. Richard Gere, but the young version, or Hugh Jackman with a barely-controllable beard, always looking like Mom just died, but sturdy and kempt, ready to throw that love into the next doe-eyed sensitive thing that needs caring and a back-scratch.

"I love it, don't you, Teddy?" X says, changing the subject, admiring how the light filters through the blinds directly into about the one spot we would logically put a couch.

"I don't know, honey. Too much sunlight really bothers Smoke when he's got a hangover."

"Well is Smoke moving in with *us*?" X is sarcastic, grinning, making eyes with the realtor like they were in some communal clitoris-possessing joke about the robust cluelessness of man.

"I haven't asked him yet, but I bet he'd consider."

Things are going, and some dough, a bit, adult-ish almost, is at-hand. Accounts are far from the red, cupboards are full of pasta, late night pizzas can currently be ordered without a balance-checking phone call, without fingers crossed—Smoke and I looking at each other with glassy eyes, thinking, then knowing, this was our last chance for salvation, for slosh-stomach grease and proteins, for us to each pass out on our respective couches, an opened but unfinished beer bottle apiece, *Goodfellas* or some such thing on the TV and last cigarettes smoldering in the ashtray as our cobwebs and empty drunk dreams creep through the blinds with the nearing sunlight.

No need nowadays, the portfolio is currently strong: here I am, a budding writer of food, dissector of culture and roast beef gravy. Coverer of regional patois and po' boys, nuance-pointer-outer, cataloguer of local character and Leidenheimer's French rolls. Knower, of things. Currently so writerly that maybe I should get glasses? Grow a goatee? The guy, alone, at the end of the bar, but with something quite large to say, and so he'll have another.

Nearly six comments have already been posted on my brave, sweeping New Orleans story: one pending moderation, but I'm sure it will be a zinging endorsement from Smoke, seeing as how I offered a six-pack in repayment. There's my mom's, and there's one from Ike, which maybe doesn't count because there are no words, only his screen name—*slobmyknob*—which means he was just registering, trying to figure out the internet, almost got it, and then hit Return a bit too soon. Which means three unrelated people have read the piece, at least partially, taken time out of their busy day of corporate slavedom and social media to scroll down, all the way, through the editor-insisted-upon pictures, and were moved sufficiently to post, in order:

"Nice."

"I make $50 an hour online secret shopping. Ask Me HOW!"

"Weak f*cking list."

Finding that asterisk is no easy task, I applauded the gumption of the reader to seek it and locate it, to keep his or her heartfelt profanity publishable.

As per usual, my successes come back in haunting waves. Much like Proust – you think he could go out to eat after "Swann's Way" without proprietors heaping fruits and hoagies upon him, hoping he would go off on some tantric spell and write the greatest review in the history of Yelp, or order the entirety of the menu in reckless revelry-laced abandon? Nonetheless, a decision to make, of the adult variety, now sits in front of my face, softish hard-wooded, currently under my boots, and it is true what they say about decisions being like assholes, or however that one goes. X is asking what I'm mumbling to myself and nodding reassuringly to our house-shower, I know expecting something from me, the right comment, the step-up, the decisiveness of Stalin, or Jim Kelly, the leading hero she always knew was inside that slightly fat guy with the Bills hat and splotchy sideburns. I do my best, clear my throat, smile, glance to my ex-girlfriend, now-fiancé, back to the suit, and head for the bathroom, saying, "I'm just gonna quick check the flushing power."

9. BOCCE CLUB PIZZA
4174 Bailey Ave.
Buffalo, NY 14226

The thesis, the framework, the entire jumping off point, like the shuttle launch pad down in Florida (though not for the one that broke apart on national television and killed the high school teacher), would be the pepperoni. The way it curls, cups, and pools, acting as not only progenitor of pizza topping grease but also as vessel, burly, wide-shouldered *deliveryman*, all in one.

It's a kind of miracle of animal protein, but not the "craft" kind, not the "artisanal" crock-of-the-moment type, not of the bearded fetishists unable to make art school pay for a contented mainstream life, those who romanticize themselves with tattoos and close-mindedness and strict over-obsession on vintage archaich-ness in their talismans of the everyday.

It's a hot dog, dick.

But I've topped it with housemade kimcheee!

Is housemade like homemade?

Yes, but, well, it's housemade…

Is a house like a home? Is a condo like an apartment?

I don't… I don't understand…

8 bucks!? A piece?!

Yes, well…

I'll take 2.

It's just pepperoni, what's always been bought here, not free-range, as inorganic as possible, *processed*, hopefully, and of the naturally curling varietal that blackens around the edges and gives off its own fat in little puddles that it then catches itself, to bring toward the mouth hole, to splash around on the tongue and counterpoint the saltiness of the nickel-shaped love button. If not healthy, you'd still have to figure these cows or pigs died *happy* — massaged, beer-drunk, cigarettes after meals, a lot of TV with feet up on coffee tables, properly gorged. Stuffed to death, perhaps, on Mighty Taco burritos.

I used to wonder about the craftsmanship back there amongst the many rows of ovens. Rolling up Bailey to Bocce's in my father's pickup, riding shotgun on a night that seemed like the biggest of the year, like Christmas Eve and the 4th of July thrown together, with a sprinkling of MLK Day for proper gravity. It was generally, probably, mostly just a random Tuesday when Mom didn't feel like cooking, or the old man was too happy-hour blitzed to want to go out, his buzz already established, drinking through dinner from the plush free-ness of the fridge a far better option, like the holidays after all, and there was little Teddy, wide-eyed, pre-boner, greasy palms, wearing clothes that don't fit, his feet pointing inward at angles when he walks, thinking himself the grandest little tyke this side of the Niagara, with big notions and a bigger appetite. Barely able to see over the counter but more happy to sense the workings, the grindings, the dough tosses, the ovens, extending back, forever. Creating the smell, thick, the heat layers explaining the counter man's pit stains, those dark circles on a gray tee hinting at ardor, blue-collar toil, Sisyphean struggle with the wooden pizza peel, but belying his easiness with Pops.

"Taking out?"

"Taking out."

"How's things?"

"Looking up, now."

"Can't get enough, eh?"

"The old lady craves your pepperoni."

"Ahh…"

"Think this little guy does too."

And I'd look up—how small we seem in memories—relish the thickness of dad's beard from my so-inconsequential-we-can-discuss-him-in-front-of-his-face wee-one perch below the counter. Not concerned about the words they were sharing, or what dad meant with one finger quick in-n-outing the circle he was forming with the index and thumb of his other hand. I was too busy dreaming big, wondering if each pepperoni was hand-sculpted by some Sicilian back there, out of sight, with a ponytail and dark penetrating eyes, like the fellas on the cover of those paperbacks Mom was always leaving on the back of the toilet. Maybe with a cigarette in his mouth, a sense of cleanliness or health department standards not yet formed in my nascent prefrontal cortex.

I wondered if he had a special, crescent-shaped axe with which he would hand-carve each slice into little bowl-like contraptions. Or if he cut them straight, picked up the thick red meat token in two palms, and then gently rolled the edges until basin-like body was achieved. The care he must take, the passion, how he'd hold each up to the light to inspect structural integrity, and how the boss, eyes always on the bottom line, would rush him, "C'mon Antonio, c'moooon." How cool he'd be, unfettered, with the silly pride of an organ grinder, the attention to detail, an ignorance for Machiavellian capitalist pushing, adherence to the way his father taught him *his* father's techniques, filial pride, memories of their little seaside Mediterranean village, the water blue and the wind soft. A reluctance to sacrifice art, craft, soul, for expedited versions of the 14-inch Tuesday Night Special pies of Tonawanda, Buffalo, New York. The dreams and tender folly of youth.

And what is that wonder? For the pizza of youth? Of *your* youth? Everyone with the, "You've never had pizza until you've had" fill in the blanks. The, "There's this place, in St. Louis..." with that faraway look in their eye, recalling. Or, "Someday I'm going to bring you..." with deep seriousness in timber. Or the more aggressive variation, "I can't believe you've never tried this slice in Omaha..." We should just say, each of us fat Americans, "Crazy coincidence, you're not gonna believe this, but, as fate has it, out of the entirety of the world, I just happen to have been born within 5 miles of the best pizza place in history."

Like masturbation styles, pizza is a deeply personal thing. Everyone's got their favorite place, a name, maybe not even Italian, maybe not even a proper noun, that when they were kids and their parents had tired of them—their big mouths, the private-part exposing, the affinity for bodily functions and the related bed of punchlined jokes, and the endless, ceaseless appetites, one after another, like you're watching a marathon, day in and out—would just break down and meekly offer the word: Jimmy's. Luigi's. Ned's. Whatever. And the chorus would go up—that idiot high-pitched echo of dickheaded toddler-dom, exploding around the living room with chubby celebratory limbs raised above heads. Or maybe it was just what Mom placated you and your older brother with when it was time for her to take her own revenge on the nightlife scene that laid claim to her husband, and she knew you'd be happy with, "I left a 20 on the table." Either way, the nostalgia never fades, the perfect combo of cooked carbs, tomato carnage, liquefied cheese goop or close-enough substitute, and, hopefully, some meat. The comfort therein is central to our formative personhood, like potty training or failed Super Bowl memories, irremovable from the happy wide-eyed moments that have added up to our collected bag of attitudes, opinions, and strong-willed takes on the world.

Unfortunately, everyone not raised within Dad's drunk-driving distance of Bocce's is wrong. Everyone that can't take in halftime of a Bills game from within back-of-the-hand-on-the-top-of-the-box-it's-still-warm territory has been misguided and lied to.

Even Grandma agrees, as she freely throws down for Bills game deliveries.

"Make it rain, Grandma!"

"Is this how?" She mimes what Johnny and I have been teaching her, right hand fanning crisp twenties out of the left, old lady bills sprinkling and wafting down to the carpet as she giggles and Johnny nearly spit takes.

She risks everything—the fact that the driver will know where she lives, that he's probably a minority and a criminal, will come back later that night, or rather a few nights later, he doesn't want to be predictable, plus he probably needs plotting time, and maybe the help of another fellow, equally degenerate, with more tattoos and darker skin, to pillage her endless supply of white envelopes full of cash and violate and trample her shocked, lifeless heap of a body, and she'll die in the hall, violated, left a mushy stump of humanity, going for the pepper spray in which drawer she can never quite remember.

It's a gamble somehow worth it, for that bright gravy and the thick-cut pepperoni bowls that make you glad you were born a meat-eater, as they say, and grateful Dad could always find his way there and back despite eight or more drinks. Though she's only permitted one slice, even Grandma can see that. Through her cataracts, through her 80-something dementia and death-gazing, through her home invasion fear—"*Nobody's* gonna wanna take advantage of ya, Grandma!" the common refrain from Johnny, "I'm not so sure…" my response, looking her up and down—through an apprehension of the world and strangers, a timidity well-honed since O.G. Johnny's earthly departure.

When Bocce's comes, with a *vvrrroooom* and a brake grind, always bad brakes with these guys, and after the realization that it's not a church friend stopping over, that it's no car breaking down in front of the house, and after reading the placard on the roof signifying deliverance (Johnny acting as front-line scout, relishing the announcement, pacing beforehand, back and forth, reminding us, palms out, pleading, conciliatory, urging all, "Be calm, it'll be here, be calm"), there is no death, there is no dread. There is only life, and delicious, grease-bathed living.

10. BUFFALO (5-4)

Blue Monday People.

The sun is puny in the face of the gray, whooshing Buffalo wind, walloping Molson cans like so many tumbleweeds down Sheridan. The neighbors-stomping-upstairs headache is substantial, but somehow less compared to a more deliberate, unkillable weekend fatigue. Liver pains are mostly in the mind, I tell myself, with a cocktail of feigned bravery and mild annoyance, distracted as per usual with dialed-up scores from around the league, swatting at brain cobwebs like the real cobwebs of forgotten basement corners.

I'm sitting at Jim's again, shameless, this being the daytime shift, after all. Grandma's ride is in the parking lot while my phone and an open notebook sit splayed in front of me on the table. I stare at futile empty pages like a Wild West dual, noting that they could come in handy should I not pick up enough napkins on the way back from the counter, or should I take an overly avuncular bite of ribeye and need to jot down a plea for Heimlich help. At the same time there's a buzz in the back of my brain that I mistake for a ringing phone every time I turn my head just so, which I do, frequently, checking the oily-skinned kid with no arm hair at the flattop. Spacing, craggily wondering where employers find kids with such spatula skill. Is there some kind of draft? Is there a fantasy league I could start?

Ike, you got the second pick.

Tell you who I'm not taking. Motherfucking drive-in girl at Mighty you got such an over-boner for.

Do I ask? Over-boner...?

An over-boner is when it's so erect that it stands too close to the body. Can't get shit done with that. And I bet she's got chlamydia from all that beef anyhow.

It gives you chlamydia?

Where else would I have gotten it?

I hope he doesn't notice me fawning, mouth agape with a dead-eyed dehydrated stare, looking and yearning with the stomach, food voyeurism at its meatiest, it's deepest and emptiest and most depraved. Today's hunger has a moany bent of desperation, like a wounded animal backed into a garage corner, or like an animal that had too many whiskies with their too many beers last night. I'm thankful to be here, and curious how such hangover-killing shamans exist in such humble, corporeal forms. How they float among us in insouciant baseball caps, and study at night, and don't yearn for accolades of the foodie, beardish, *Bon Apetit* variety—that lot of stiff-aproned posers of calorie-creation. I'm also curious if I should have gotten three side beef tacos instead of two, my stomach lost in gurgling wonder along with me.

My head is doing the ringing again, and I need to turn around. It's not just the sound of spinal fluid filtering its way through the belabored brain stem, either: this time, alerted by the blinking and that weird shimmying that signifies society's full acceptance of the presence of vibrators in everyday life, even on tables where food is to be consumed, it's actually my phone.

"Are you having a nice time, sweetie?" Mom asks, undermining the seriousness of intent, my professionalism, the fact that I picture myself with an old derby on, PRESS written on an index card popped in the brim. Always with a hot lead, a scoop on the councilman, chain-smoking and hurrying toward a row of pay phones, a half-empty bottle of brown liquor in my bottom desk drawer for late nights of objective poetry that will rock the city at dawn.

"Grueling. Ya *know*, work?" As if she had forgotten what that was, or that it was something with which I only occasionally flirted. As if, also, I was asking her, asking if this counted toward that thing she always warned me of, that big bad bully, reality, the one at the end of all that pubescent idealizing and pot-smoking and masturbation and Kerouac.

"Ohh, how's all that?" She's affecting a Midwestern twang in her voice, so innocent sounding, seemingly done to annoy me, annoyance often seeming to be her thing.

"Deadline's creeping up."

"Are Ike and Johnny getting along?"

"Not really."

"Are they being nice to you?"

"Ike throat punched some guy at Caputi's, almost got me killed."

"Somebody say something about OJ?"

"No. Super Bowl, I think."

"Which one?"

"Doesn't matter."

"He still give you grief that you didn't cry enough?"

That's when I spot her: in line with her back turned, wearing those pants that are in some sort of style nowadays. The ones that say *I'm into yoga, Whole Foods, being a fashionable woman-on-the-go, Nalgene bottles for my water, voting for a woman president,* and, also, *look at my butt.* She may seem drastically out of place, what with the sunlight, this being the wrong side of Sheridan and there being no thick partition for drink-holding and elbow-leaning standing between us, but it's her, definitely, Ms. Jameson from Caputi's, of white tank top notoriety, in line for a chicken finger sub.

"I gotta go, Mom."

"Is it diarrhea?"

"No, it's the boss, on the other line, call-waiting."

"Tell him he should let you have some more stuff published, you're stuff's been so gooood." Always with too many vowels, the upward lilt on the word, like religious music, resolving to the major, picking you up.

"You want me to tell my boss that my mom says I should get more assignments?"

"Yeeeaaah, and more words."

"Noted. More assignments and more words. I'll let him know Mom says."

"Ok. Love you hon…"

I hang up, clearing the line for the fake phone conversation that needs to take place. She gets her number from the counter and turns with her empty cup for water, looking for a place to plop said yoga pants, looking so tired, while our mutual benefactor does his cheese-gooping life's work and charity. I put my cup to my mouth, thinking my profile in drinking might expedite the recognition phase, before returning the phone to my ear.

Token fake phone conversation:

"Yeah, I don't know, I got a flight to Laguardia." (Worldly)

"…"

"Oh you know, she'll pick me up." (Planting jealousy seeds)

"…"

"Someplace, in the East Village, I think." (Successful, baller, but laid back, Bohemian, go-with-the-flow and so forth)

"…"

"Yeah, I'll be in Brooklyn that night, we can go to that Ethiopian tapas place if you want." (Wizened, hip, accommodating)

"…"

"Can you pick up that thing for me?" (Mysterious, Bond, or a bad boy with an edge, like Javier Bardem might play, or somebody with such complex-toned skin and brooding eyes)

She makes her way past my table and there I sit, there's Teddy, with a play-it-cool grin and scrunched-up eyebrows, interrupting his fake conversation, holding his phone away for a second. I cock my head questioningly to the side, and I'm doing the finger wag thing—at her person, then at mine—as if to ask, "Do we know each other?" Slyly, Englishly, like Cary Grant might in black and white, though I don't even know if he's English. She's busy looking at her phone though, doesn't notice me on the way past, doesn't look up until she's seated, and then I note she's got eyes for the beef guru, too—locking in on him, maybe avoiding me. Hangover hunger might make sense for her, too, seeing as how I bought her at least a couple shots last night. I maintained a level head through the "Can I buy you a shot?" process, mostly, I think, though trying to remember now an uncertainty makes the blood vessels in my face do their overheating bit.

I pretend I was counting something on my fingers, try to cover up my gesticulating toward flirtation that went ignored, but maybe I've given up that power, that coolness, the one that comes from being a lone wolf at a bar in a strange city, with no bits of recognition. The brooding type, the not-sure-about-that-guy-at-the-end-of-the-bar guy, tortured, burdened, always smoking solo and staring at the stars and devil-may-caring. That may have washed away with my attempt at connection, may currently be replaced in the minds of my fellow midday cheesesteak connoisseurs, them now likening me to the overly-avuncular police-sketch sort.

I picture it all going down, anyways...

"I'm a writer," I'd say, bowing, almost hovering, but not in a reach-for-the-mace way. Like she asked, and now we're in on a secret together. "A *food* writer."

All it takes, to begin. Something mellow, grooving—JJ Cale, early Dire Straits, Jeff Lynne, acoustic-driven and nostalgic, but neither weepy or self-conscious—kicks in as we get up and make for the door with mild, sheepish grins at one another. I'd dangle my keys at arm's length, like you might with a dog, affably, humorously, and somehow I'm the guy in the erectile dysfunction medication commercial, and then I'm holding the door, gallant, just as our to-be-decided soundtrack singer starts to croon about something long past and underappreciated. But what's this? Could it be? Ms. Jameson is the one that remembers, thinking about it, a bit embarrassed, but yes, ah ha, of course, *let's get some tacos for the road!* Quick, back to the counter, and then we're outside and it's just when the drums hit.

Cruising west, and then south, she's unwrapping a beef taco. "Spicy," she says, "for you," making with the eyes, cupping it with her her left hand and moving it toward me, peeling back the wrapper with her right. I lean forward, a bit to the right, hands on the wheel, and she sticks it in. Deep. A big bite. A bit of glistening spit still connected as she pulls it away, the strand getting thinner, not wanting to let go. I turn my eyes back on the road, embarrassed, face turning red. But, wait, what was that? Did she just break my saliva streak with her hand? I feel a tingling, loins warm, blood rushing a bit, but she just laughs and rolls down the window, like it's warm out. I note her familiarity with the rolling kind of window—no fancy modern button-operated stuff for O.G. Johnny! And she's hanging on my every word, first about fat content in grass fed beef, and then New Orleans, the genius of it, my recent story and how this piece flowed out organically—"I'm sorry for using the word 'organically'"—from my south-set novel. I'm shrugging my shoulders, in an *aww schucks* type of way, deflecting, "whatever"-ing, playing it cool, but passionately speaking with my hands and going deep, and she keeps smiling, prodding. Now she's asking about Grandma and her cheesy scrambled eggs.

"Have I told you?"

"I heard you last night at the bar. I was eavesdropping. Ha! I'd love to meet her."

"She's great. Deserves none of the credit, it's all about the Velveeta, really, but, yeah, she's great."

Neither of us seems to know where we're going. I tune to 97 Rock and Billy Gibbons greets us both with a *har har har har*, and at this she smiles brighter, and I smile brighter for seeing her smile brighter, until we're beaming love poem ferocious, all meat-breath and smoky, dwarfing the Buffalo gray as we loop by the sad ghosts of a north side university.

"My dad went here."

"My dad went here!"

This is the funniest thing in the world to her. There's a former mental hospital, sprawling, disjointed, macabre, abandoned, in the middle of our collective fathers' college campus, and now, with this company, it takes on a downright cheery hue, even though there are drops of rain and rolling cloudiness. She goads me further, "No, keep going," like she's playing at Nancy Drew, her eyes getting big, emboldening me, awakening dormant machismo. We note the broken-out windows, the coming storm, the obvious horror movie setting we're taking on here, but she's reaching into the plastic bag, me having almost forgotten about the extra calories in our midst, the combination almost too much, despite the greasy beef smell now permeating the car. "I almost forgot. I got you something!" With a Christmas-morning smile, the kind like when you are gifting the perfect present—the season-opener tickets for Dustin, the James Taylor for Mom, the freeze dried Mighty Tacos for Johnny— she pulls out a clear plastic container: jalapeno wedges!

Then we're moving on, stopping to get coffee at a spot on Elmwood. The sun has come out after a downpour and I put on my fake Ray Bans. She lights my cigarette as we walk back toward the car and tells me she likes my Bills hat, how it's great I didn't go for a throwback logo like the lot of vintage-chasers, them always looking back, always driving in reverse. She's fascinating, going on with her metaphor, something about a looming sore neck and your arm falling asleep, what with the weird way you have to cock it behind the passenger side headrest to keep looking out the back window.

Suddenly we're stopped in the shadows of Central Terminal, night beginning to fall, the abandoned train station coming to life with rats, probably. The neighborhood feels funky, edgy, but the trespassing and the joint we just smoked hold no sway over a surprising cool-heeled confidence. Tom Petty is even playing, acoustic, talking of bad boys, and I'm nodding, doing the head-tilting thing necessary when eating tacos while driving, extra care taken to not lose any hot sauce.

I'm sharing my jalapenos, and she plops them right on the head of her taco, taking one whole with each bite and fanning her mouth a bit, then grinning over at me, sideways. Looking immaculate, the seatbelt separating, pronouncing, each breast.

"See what I did with these? I even asked for extra seeds!"

We have a kid, later, but he dies. It's one night, shortly after little Jimbo is born, when we're out at this real foodie small-plate joint, hottest table in town—duck confit flautas, Yelpers, repurposed wood, mason jars. I have a big assignment and we're making a date night out of it. Treating ourselves, for the work of having a child, for becoming parents, throwing down for a babysitter, getting drunk, cheersing our good fortune. Then little Jimbo tumbles out the window—unlocked from me sneaking a bathroom smoke, even after I swore to give up smoking once we became parents. Or maybe it's just SIDS, inexplicable, nobody's fault but God's. Either way, she never forgives me, and from that point forward each of us has a hard time eating, the passion gone, even for pizza. The big denouement comes when I walk in on her mawing a Dominos', the kind with the crust stuffed with cheese. I'm furious, understandably, but she's bawling, and there's even sausage on it as a topping, and she screams, "But what difference does it make!?" I hurl a slice against the wall with great manly malice, and it sticks, for a moment, the camera closing up on it and then sliding over to a little framed picture of Jimbo, and then back to the Dominos' moist cardboard crust plopping loudly to the kitchen tile floor.

"What are you doing to yourself!? To US!?" I scream, crying, and she's crying, too, and the strings are playing and heartstrings are being yanked with manipulative fervor…

It all finishes, our movie, just in time for my guy to finish another soft-rolled masterpiece, to add another notch in his magnum. He looks questioningly at this audience and despondently shouts, "Number 77!"

before turning back to his canvas.

The movie will draw rave reviews from a couple of major city alternative weeklies, become widely-respected and a-couple-times-nominated on the minor film festival circuit. It will even develop a kind of cult following in some eastern Midwest private colleges, where there are film *classes* but no real *film department*, and the kids are smart, but only kind of.

"I like to get my blue cheese on the side, too," I say, back to reality, finding some fortitude and going for it on my way back from the counter, hoagie and tacos in hand.

"Huh?" she asks.

"Allows you to unevenly distribute, ya know?"

"I'm sorry?"

"Sometimes you want a really blue cheesy bite, sometime a more hot sauce-centric one. Good to alternate."

I'm nodding at her, referencing her order, the one I overheard and admired, trying to get through, but it's like I'm speaking Greek and my jowls are beginning the glow, and not like in the movie. It's obstinate, foreign, like there's mashed potatoes in my cheeks and my tongue is stropping.

"I know you, don't I?" She's not smiling, just searching. I notice her eyes are brown, not green like in the directorial debut of my mind. She also has something of a double chin. A thing we'll have to work on, or rather leave in, verisimilitude being something these days.

"You poured me something like four shots of Jameson last night."

"You were with That Guy. The burly fucker. The puncher." Her potty-mouth seemed more attractive in the screen test, now it mostly just sounds like she's from Tonawanda.

"I'm sorry. My uncle. Thing is," I look around, lowering my voice, "he drinks."

"Is that the thing?"

There's a palpable awkwardness. I wait for her to tell me not to come back—"Not to Caputi's, not even to Jim's!"—it all her tight-panted domain now, the glorious gastronomic trail of Sheridan Avenue. With nothing to lose, then, but more burst capillaries, I push on.

"You ever need a ride to work, see that Malibu out yonder? It's my grandma's."

"Ohhh. Blue, eh? Very nice."

"Yep. I can get it almost whenever I want."

"I bet you can."

Our mutual friend calls her order number—"78!"—and she smiles as she brushes by, on her way to the sandwich, to happiness, to that impossible new-math calculus of meat, cheese and loaf, coming together in tongue-banging fusion.

"Bruuuuuce. Nice."

"Huh?" She stops, puzzled.

"Bruuuuuce."

"Uhh...?"

"Bruce Smith. Number 78. Not bad. Good sandwich omen."

"Well..." Nudging past me now a bit, smiling, looking down.

I turn to watch her butt go past. Then, lowly, inspired by thought of the baddest Bill of all-time, I let one more go, like it's 1990 and O.G. Johnny is there, air-punching, in demand for yet another beat-down, another sack: "Bruuuuuuuce."

Calling an audible, feeling this is the exit, the leave on a high note moment and this a sandwich for the privacy of Grandma's, I reach into my bag, pull out my side container of jalapeno slices, pop the top, pull out a big one, with a bunch of seeds, and place it square in the center of the logical eating spot on the table in front of her chair. A calling card, an amulet, a dream-catcher, and I pop my sunglasses on and hit the door without a look back, the sandwich bag dangling by my side.

11. CHICAGO (0-0)

"Let's just go back to New Orleans, man," Smoke says, liberally packing the pipe. "We'll get a place. Fuck this shit."

Fuck this shit being our primary exclamation point, and period, too, for such a conversation—a State of the Union conversation, currently taking place amidst smoke billows and cloudy end-of-the-week rationale. Smoke is pontificating as he packs, getting going, loosening and pushing up the Friday work shirt sleeves, almost crazed, a bit earlier than normal, a bead of sweat appearing now at his temple, it seems. Neil Young or some such business is currently pulsing from the speakers on the floor, behind which a not-small amount of dust bunnies scurry about in wattage-amplified discontent.

Our couch ass grooves are getting right, warm, weekend-familiar, and he's becoming a bit sloppy, avuncular, agitatedly spilling some leafiness around the table, then on the floor. He takes out a stem and sticks it in his mouth—something to chew, to let hang like a farmer with straw in his mouth, while he works his thumbs over the glassware. I notice, in a sort of from-the-other-side-of-the-glass-at-the-zoo view, patiently waiting with a beer in hand, how he's emboldened by carelessness, like drunkards so often are, *fuck it*, when they grow a late night disdain for coasters, for anything *straight* or *mainstream*, and get that notion for *I'll tell ya somethings*, always punctuated with an extended, pointed index finger.

"Alls I know, is, fuck, this is fucked…"

"It's funny, this really came about because you said you were moving out." I push, needle, resting my chin in my palm like an expensive analyst. Then I take a swig.

"See, that's what I'm saying." He's talking with his hands now, underlining and subtly backhanding each individual point. "Why does moving have to be such a big deal? Leases, commitment, shit."

"I'm pretty sure it's not a lease when you buy a house."

"Excuse me, I didn't realize you had your realtor's license. Didn't know about your moonlighting gig as a fucking land surveyor. Didn't know you were some kind of property assessor, Mr. Mainstream."

His voice goes up at the end of each sentence, jocular but accusatory, a bit bleary, throaty, chesty, very physical, from some place south of the lips. The truth is I don't know about leases, or home-ownership, or how one affects the other. Why movement toward such commitments is always, ubiquitously, to be celebrated. Movement in general it seems, the clack-clack of heels on pavement, a wake in the mainstream, is somehow universally agreed to be the right act.

But, currently, I'm just after the standard rigmarole of juiced-up jostling, the inexorable male potion of Friday nights, no matter the season or topic, or the coming death of it all. He'd be pointing again by now, but his hands are otherwise occupied, trying to get us both high. Helping to assuage the malignant cell reproduction of adulthood happening all around us. Meanwhile I'm keeping my head about me, level, like Morgan Freeman after bad news, someone has to be strong, *be strong, dammit*, chin up and tough, with clear-eyed head nods in the direction of what needs to be done, despite the handful of IPAs floating through the bloodstream. The beer is running ragtag posse-like with the two large-ish happy hour bowls Smoke packed to get me in my ass groove and brace for the big bad talk ahead. The one everybody knew was coming—the cat included, but him not caring, still mostly just concerned with his clammy anus—it being what's coming everywhere around us. The standard business of the late-20s in-between world of fiancés, houses, and such. Purgatory, really, us all moving toward suburban despondency, toward nice-couch complacency, comfortable placation if you're lucky, kids if you're crazy, and the eventual diagnosis, most likely, or old age, and the relapse to the point in your life of who-cares contentedness, where you can't bend down low enough and don't mind near enough to clean the underpart of the toilet.

The side bit of business to such progress, for Smoke and I, is that of breaking up.

"Well, one more big fling, then, before the divorce. Like break-up sex, eh? Ehhhh?"

At this he's actually nudging my arm with his elbow, looking for a bailout, offering me the pipe. I tell him he's being kind to him-self, but I know that's not the truth. He's breaking both our hearts, all our hearts, because the cat, Smoke, and I all know he doesn't really want to go. There's far too many late-night conversations in the bank for any excited talk of mortgage rates or "settling down" to be believed.

By this point I'm doing that thing where I hold a half-smoked Camel between the index and middle fingers of my left hand, the bowl between my thumb and palm, the lighter in my right hand and a full beer sweating less than an arm's length away. Somehow I always picture my mother at these times, and my grandmoth-er, too. That kind of if-they-could-see-me-now bit of abandon, or maybe stupidity, that Fridays for the past decade have come to be about. Saturdays, too. Smoke even once deemed it my "Statue of Liberty" play, it being somehow reminiscent of great things, nobil-ity, grandeur, forthcoming pontificating about justice, art, and our collective manhood. The kind of moment worthy of a statue. It's one of the inside jokes we forget to keep going, probably something to do with the circumstances from which it generally arrives.

"How about Buffalo? You wanna go to Buffalo instead?"

I take a deep swill of Sierra and sit back, let the smoke swirl toward the dusty fan that we could turn on if we cared, letting it all wash over me, wishing we could skip back on the CD to the part about the burned out basement, it feeling more appropriate, but I don't want to harsh Smoke's, mine, the cat's, newfound mellow. Also, the CD player remote is broken.

"We could stay at Grandma's, maybe. She gives great back scratches."

"Those cheesy scrambled eggs too, eh?" He's getting on board, sideways smiling at me as he reaches out to ash his butt.

"You watch your fucking mouth about my grandmother. Show some respect. She's not making *you* any cheese goo goos."

"C'mon, man. New Orleans. Write more New Orleans shit. It was brilliant. Brilliant."

Smoke usually only says nice things after midnight. It's a trait I catch in him and often wonder if the same applies to me. If I'll exist in someone else's novel, movie, as that guy that only says "I love you" after four drinks. But there's no maliciousness in it, just like the fiancé he says he loves, and her kid he seems to genuinely like. It's all hidden by layers, but present, like citrus essence just when you get your nails in, and never more palpable than with New Orleans, the recollection of which renders us nodding, malleable goops of nostalgia. For charbroiled oysters, for Chartres, for that corner bar jukebox and a wasted rainy afternoon, for a fog that may not have even been there, might very well be a trick of 'member when-ing, invented on an especially good rooftop night, back when we used to have the energy to climb the apartment building stairs toward the roof, light each other's cigarettes under the moon like poets, and discuss the essence of our still important mid-20s, and New Orleans, and the book I was supposed to write about our time there. About our train trip, full of solid eye contact and endless friendship-cementing, and having figured out so much, so many late-night lessons and assured creed-making on which we now seem to just rest our beers, or with which we light our unsure smokes.

He's up now, propelled by vacation good timey thought, down on his knees in front of the stereo, ass in the air, thumbing through my vinyl stack, needing something warmer. Half-listening, searching higher vibes for more bass, for more smoky synchronicity. It reminds me of a time I saw him at a party, one of those open air summer jobs where some of us feel awkward about smoking and starting to get drunk while the sun is still out because others of us have brought the whole clan and are comparing diaper brands or some such business. His fiancé's daughter had fallen, gotten one of those cuts that come from being simultaneously uncoordinated and brattish, and there was Smoke, down on both knees, setting his beer aside, disregarding instantaneously some point I was making about Jimi or chorizo and going in for a closer examination before offering the most big-hearted, "You can walk it off, Champ," anyone has ever heard. His ass in the air will always remind me of good-natured, fatherly tenderness, from the kind of father not to hide in a bathroom after a loss, once the confusion has settled in. The kind Johnny and I needed after Norwood scuffed our childish knees, and most any future chance at being. And so, not every lesson is learned in the wee hours: some people have things in them you'll never see until a crisis point at a silly Sunday cookout, with BBQ poofs blowing around a picnic table lined with ketchup and mustard and plastic silverware.

"So I have this idea," I say, beginning to talk out of my own ass and directly into another, the earlier pot-smoking losing its orbit, the beer leveling it out toward dreamy conversationality. Smoke is *mmmhuh*-ing absently, occasionally holding up a record for my vague disapproval, to which he replies with, "Ah, fuck you," and I imagine the voice coming out of his butt, which makes me smile, weak and stoned, out of the corner of my mouth, but I don't mention it and keep going.

"That pepperoni I talk about. 'Member? Kind of like the life blood pool of my family, but of the whole city, too. Grease really being the great equalizer of food. Like alcohol. The byproduct we all manage in our own way, the thing part of us all, to savor and enjoy, to fear and to be pleased by. The thing not part of any ingredient list, both appalling and enticing. Like with that po' boy joint, 'member? Eating on the paper over the hotel bed and you said gravy and mayo and hot sauce make their own blood? It's their own singular goo essence, you said. You nailed it, man." And now, lustily shaking my head, for the glory of a long past day, and meal.

"You nailed it, Smoke."

"You gonna pitch it? A pepperoni story?"

"Fuck yeah."

Like that, I feel a solid counterpunch has been landed to my own life's advancement. It's no house purchase, no defeat of cancer—in fact, I'm still struggling with a creeping ulcer or two that I've begun to wonder about. I've never been to Europe, let alone on a proper business trip, one with a per diem, travel expenses, a blazer to wear to the airport bar and a goatee on my face. I ended my college career long enough ago that I have to think, do math, count on the fingers of one hand and then use the fingers on the other before answering, "When did you graduate?" But this pitching effort is at least a bit more than last year's fantasy football runner-up finish. This one I can tell mom about with some clarity.

Oooohhh, and I didn't even know you played football, honey!

No, mom. Fantasy.

Oooh, you were always such a little dreamer.

"So you're going to write about pepperoni?" This is offered with such flat eyebrow scrunch, genuine wonder and a slight head nod on the uptake, that I wonder how I'll function without such an ally, one so robust, such an accomplice in overindulgence and the after-hours facts. Simultaneous, lurking below all this, is the coming wonder on how I'll pay rent.

It's hard to believe, but assured, that the night will end, much later, with us both up, on our feet, ass grooves de-sponging, barely, cooling, the couches getting a break before tomorrow's inevitable nap sessions. Paul Simon will play entirely too loud for the after-bar hour, for the couple of moments where I stop and put my hand on his shoulder and look at him with poetic intent and say, "You're doing the right thing." Even though he's not, and I'm pre-lost, like setting out for a new city with no map and blurring vision, but we'll mouth the words and mime all the bass solos. We'll finger-point-exclaim important lines about turnaround jump shots, air guitar some sinewy African lines, hips shaking and ashes carelessly blown about the room. Dancing will be stopped only when it's time to take a serious puff from the pipe, and then it will resume, and *fuck its* will be had. Smoke's moving out, toward something vague and inevitable, involving people and support and roofs over one's head that he'll be responsible for when a shingle blows off in a night storm. And what do you do, who do you call, when a shingle falls off? But fuck shingles, tonight we say *fuck it*, the it referring to *this shit*, as always, and I will both make and let Smoke buy the 4AM pizza—it being our last, maybe, as he moves to a new place, neither New Orleans nor Buffalo, unknown, and certainly not as fun as either.

12. ANCHOR BAR
1047 Main St.
Buffalo, NY, 14209

Mom never really invented anything. There *was* that strange after-dinner treat, more a fruit trick in the guise of dessert, with banana, milk, and sugar. She'd slice up banana wedges and let them float and sink through a bowl of semen-textured white liquid with a sprinkling of sugar poured from one of those glass canisters every American house used to have, this back before it was discovered that sugar gives us cancer and, worse, makes us fat. Strangely satisfying, soothing more than anything else, it was like a childhood nightcap, coating and readying the gut for sleep. I've long thought to try to recreate the dish, spiked with some rum or something more fit for adulthood, but the ratios always throw me. There's also the fact that bananas, once inescapable, ubiquitous in any abode run by Mom, happened to stop being around once I was paying my own rent and buying my own pizzas. I never noticed that bananas don't come with the wallpaper until around age 25.

Or, actually, for more than a while it seemed Mom wanted credit for coming up with the "20 on the table" ritual. Neither Johnny nor I ever felt the need to correct her, lest we detract from the greatest promise childhood seemed to yield. But the way she'd say it, interrupting a backyard O.J. reenactment—the stiff arm, the down-the-sideline sprint, picturing myself in those gigantic shoulder pads, glimpsing the whole thing in black-and-white, the way that O.G. Johnny would look at films of the Juice with that slight head shake, with disbelief and awe, like he'd never seen anything like it, his own Fred Jackson, but better; or me in Johnny's headlock, for whatever reason, him choking out my little personage with the inward pointing toes but expanding gut—she'd be there in the doorway with a hand on her hip, as if to ask, with great authoritative moxie,

"Who's the best mom *and* the best chef?"

Except with Bocce's down the street, she had a perpetual ace in the hole, Mom-hood simplified: move to Tonawanda and spurt out of your uterus two fat sons that would rather have pepperoni than candy, drugs, or girls.

These are Mom's major contributions to the gastrointestinal legacy of Johnny, country club guitar hero of greater central Ohio, and Ted, who's made a couple bucks waxing poetic on calories. Hindsight also shows that she taught us how cool, how lyrical, it is to smoke that first cigarette with that first drink on an early-summer evening. "Just to scare away the mosquitoes," she'd say, a lesson years in the backpack, for darker adulthood days, when we were old enough to know what we were doing was wrong, and old enough to do it anyway.

Some stories never get passed on, of course. No need for mention of the fish stick phase, or to dwell upon the brief obsession with Sunday night spaghetti, when a boyfriend with lots of chest hair introduced her to San Marzano tomatoes and feigned an interest in the Bills to get my brother and me on his side. And also, later, to parlay said networking as a means into my mother's pants, and, seemingly, her stack of pizza-getting 20's.

"Can you get us playoff tickets?" Johnny asked one day.

I'd like to say it was me that came up with the exam, but my older brother deserves his blitz-stopping due. Chest Hair skirted the question with a good natured laugh and some head-patting condescension, but he didn't, couldn't, last long past the emasculation. To say one thing of Johnny, he'll kick you square in the nuts and never break eye contact.

On the other hand are the stories that get told too much, such as what we have here, with the Anchor Bar and its infamous bit of innovation. As the official version of the tale goes, Frank Bellissimo got a misshipment (from the most gloriously history-changing UPS man ever, probably hungover, certainly profound and misunderstood in his day, maybe even fired, such is the lack of justice lashed upon non-conformists and fuck-ups in black-and-white times), looked down at the box (wooden, needing to be opened with one of those crowbars that men of antiquity always have within arm's reach), scrunched up his furry gray eyebrows, scratched his gut through a stained white tee, started to get mad, chomped some more on his cigar, scratched his brow, and forced his wife, Teressa Bellissimo, to come up with something. It was 1964.

A sad, soulless story, that one, missing character, arc, or anything with some narrative hot sauce. It might seem to have as much hope of finding a New York publisher as the mostly sad, slightly-soulless manuscript currently taking up a 12x8 plot on the floor next to my writing desk. It's a story where listeners continue to nod their head after the teller is done, past the punchline, still wondering "Yeah? And?" Waiting for the twist, the irony, for the *A-ha!* denouement that came to be, wait for it, *chicken wings.*

Good stories never end this way. Uncle Ike stories certainly don't, and if the moon is right, and he's contentedly plopped at the kitchen table at Grandma's, beers procured, waiting in the fridge, the equivalent of a savings account and security blanket at once, his sentimentality ripened, tongue and joviality goaded, he'll go into it.

"John Young." He always starts off, simply, declaratively, the implied *you don't know the rest?* the appetizer, the whistle-whetter, the side of celery to dunk in the blue cheese.

"Isn't that the Mormon guy?" (I have variations on this, including: "Fullback, right?")

"Yeah, the Mormon guy, but they're not related."

"No?"

"Teddy, open your fucking eyes. Look at what black people down South eat."

"Collard Greens?"

"Don't be a racist."

Around this, his eyes generally start to get wide. He'll enunciate with a forefinger, the very one curling over the neck label of a sweating bottle of Molson, and he will go on as if I'd never heard the story, as if he's telling it to himself, and to Grandma, as she piddles about over the stove, tinkering with housework, cleaning, straightening, whatnot, but really keeping an eye on him, a tally on how many beers are being swilled, profanities leveled, disrespects paid.

Ike's story, consistent or not, dependent on inebriation level and hunger, has an outline, bullet points to always hit: Breaded. Fried. Some mysterious, tomato-based 'Mambo' sauce. Fried chicken bits as Southern black food. Eventually, he will tie everything to today, somehow: "This is long before Ms. Thing started slinging her ass and the Caputi's kitchen wares for Helka's 20s." There's always a kind of implied *my boy* after these guided tours of Buffalo history, the head-patting, *Story Time* kind, like a great goodnight sendoff.

But by this point, at the bartendress' very mention, the image of that wing-and-beer-bringing silhouette through those kitchen doors, we generally begin to grow our own hunger and start thinking about trudging back across Sheridan. In the wake of such history, Ike insists on ordering 'Mambo' sauce, us both breaking up, as the bartender in her tank top smiles, uncertain, and turns to punch the buttons on the cash register, digitally calling back to the unseen kitchen maestro and then scooting out of ear shot so Ike and I can aggressively clink bottles in our order-placed anticipatory glow. Over coffee the very next day, Grandma, in her nightgown, sans teeth, usually gives her own take.

"Ike tells a different story, Grandma."

"That motherless son just hates women!"

"Ike is a misogynist, agreed."

"Don't use words like that, Teddy."

"Words like what? Ike?"

"It was a holy day, Teddy. Holy."

"Good Friday, right?"

"That's right."

"Didn't something bad happen on Good Friday? Really bad. Like, the worst? Isn't that an ironic name!?"

"Don't get smart."

"I heard her son was a drunk." Always the point to stir the pot, sprinkle a bit more pepper, get the simmer up and roaring, the palpitations popping.

"Her son was a layabout, no good, that's true. But that Teressa was a saint. A *saint*, Teddy."

"What's a 'layabout'?"

"An asshole. Now, listen. It was Good Friday and everyone at the bar hadn't had any meat for all of Lent, and then, at midnight, Teressa wanted to whip up something special to break the fast."

"So that's why we always eat chicken wings at Easter?"

"No, that's because you and your brother are fat and have a problem."

Nowadays, no matter what, whoever is right, Anchor Bar is a shrine. Like Canton, as I picture it, though I don't often picture it, and don't really care to. In North Buffalo though, some kind of Latin jazz quartet sets up in the middle of the joint sometimes, and it is a happy enough spot to grab a couple of Molson's—frigidly cold, *Buffalo* cold—and set up at the bar with your elbows on the wood next to a putzy Sabres-hat-wearing schlub you could really member-when with and talk rosters and buy rounds to cancel out each other's bought rounds, until the smell overtakes your gratification delay and you order, and get your fingers all wet, soaked, and leave them like that till the end, till the period, until the ellipsis that runs toward the bathroom—but just a face-and-hand spritzing—and then the finest cigarette of all-time, the one spent gazing up at the stars, feeling the gelatinous spicy mess in your stomach coalesce into a feeling of unity, a great oneness, with all of your Buffalo forefathers.

Of course, it *would* be, could be this harmonious if not for the tourists, the gawkers, the weekend warriors from Ames, Dubuque, Iowa City, some such place where motherless masses fuck and breed and read Yelp but don't know how to keep their hands greasy throughout the eating. How they should keep the wipes for *after*. And they certainly don't know what type of oil should be used by any legit frying establishment. There's no discernment among these mouth-breathers, these mouth-fanners, them all thinking it hilarious to try, and to tell everyone back home, "I tried these *Buffalo Wings*," the emphasis all wrong, not using proper verbiage, or the proper proper nouns.

Give it a whiff, Johnny insists, on every drive past. Down Main Street, through Kenmore, away from Tonawanda, on our way to someplace he'd like to "give a whirl"—always with the whirling, of bars, and patting his gut. He'll roll down the window, throw his head back, flare the nostrils a bit, and nod like an expert. Grin knowingly at me, disappointed, but like an *it's gonna be OK* at a funeral. *We'll get through this,* he means to say, and, *all is not lost, little brother.* It's his conviction that does the job, the way I'd be certain to love Steely Dan even if I didn't, because he says so, and Johnny's expertise knows no discord, no impertinence, no room for disagreement. Except the wind does feel off as we scoot by with a couple beers already in us, Johnny assured at the wheel, the air reminding me of that mildew stench on a fresh-laundered load—how can soap cause stink? How could chicken wing grease not be the windblown essence of nirvana?—of fresh cut grass, of newly-baked Grandma-made chocolate chip cookies, that whiff of perfume in an elevator that brings you immediately back to 18-year-old backseat nights.

But so it goes, with Anchor Bar and the sainted Teressa and her layabout son. The original is something approaching one or another kind of bullshit, all old Canola and endless skating on a promise, and Mom never loved me or Johnny enough—despite our collective and incessant efforts to never be sober between the ages of 18 and the present day, to always be the ultimate layabouts—to change the world with a late-night bar snack.

This is the death of innocence we all must face, accept, embrace even, when the wind grows cold and the idols of our youth turn Disney, franchise, and get too lazy to change the fry oil, or potentially commit roughshod double homicide, and trample everything, all the promise and legend, that went before.

13. BUFFALO (5-5)

How we've all ended up back home at the same time, sans the fake cheer and frightening storms of Christmas—the usual time when modern Bills seasons lose all muster of luster and what was always false hope, and the cold and spinning-wheels slush and the getting of watery snow inside your boots and the insipid lawn ornaments make eating and drinking *more* necessary, but can also, sometimes, explain a weird sense of family togetherness—is hard to figure.

"I'm going on assignment," I fibbed, as I'd fibbed before, it coming easy and not feeling bad, like I was cutting myself in on the con, convincing myself as I heard it aloud, spoken in earnest, in that slight annoyance that one with such things to do, over and over, has to affect. One of those personality scars of adulthood and the never-ending hustle. Now that it's beginning, the never-ending-ness feels more apparent, more so probably to me than to those right in the middle of it, like a man hearing about a traffic jam, tuning in at just the right time while pulling out of his garage. Though I've yet to come upon the courage or right time to ask anyone, compare notes with those in their not-old-but-ripening vintage, those more advanced, who started earlier, while I was still tinkering with dreams and such.

Do you find yourself becoming more asshole-ish with each passing year?
Why, yes. Yes I do, now that you mention it…

"I'll help," Johnny said, when I first told him my plans. "I'll school you. I'll school that editor fuck too. Yeah, I'm there."

Johnny made it up in his mind, over the course of those first five words, gears grinding, wheels in motion, him probably getting hungry, patting the belly and disappointed in his own fridge. It was to be expected, given his insistence on moving toward a good thing and not letting work or the rent or the *What days? When?* sprinklings—necessary for advanced-stage human beings—seep into any of this potential. Gigs, rent, whatever: Grandma is there, still there, always waiting, with a car and crisp 20's, and any money worries are and should be as far away as diet plans. There is no reason to protest, though a professional, or even semi-profession- al, grown, properly-developed human with an actual assignment might offer a meek, "Well, I'll be working." Instead I smiled and said, "Can't get enough Grandma back scratches can you?"

His validation is everything my editor's mulling, pondering, chewing on, refusing to answer my email, golfing—for some rea- son I always picture him golfing, smoking a cigar in plaid pants and *har-har*-ing with some good 'ol boys while his phone rings uselessly (although I only email)—is not. But more importantly, upon first mention I at once saw big bowls of French fries between Johnny and I, in a room wood-paneled and hot-smelling, nostril-searing, the air thick with Frank's, grease remnants in third-coat thickness on the porcelain table, a plethoric stack of napkins already in front of each of us in anticipation, ignoring our sweating water glasses (unless I'm hungover already in this foresight daydream), the cold bottles of Molson easing matters, adding eagerness, whetting, and the waitress with a gut, but a winning smile, too. Johnny and I share penchants for falling in love with waitresses, his a more vocal but sheepish, vaguely charming manner.

You know I like you, but would never, ever, even think for a second about unwanted handsiness against your person. His soft smile offers reassurance, his steady, honest eye-contact met with blushes.

My approach is rendered in a much shier, grateful-type quietude.

Thank you so much. Appreciate it.

She smiles.

Thank you, thank you, and I clasp my palms together in prayer like formation, with hands and torso nodding back-and-forth in unison, in a beatific genuflection that God-fearing Helka might like, even though I don't want any more water and that's all she's pouring.

So it is that I affect the lonely scholar, searching for meaning in the way the refrieds run against the rice, finding poetry in the way the *asada* spillage comes to soft plopping rest on the table edge when it could have landed on the floor, reveling in the manner that leftover grease driblets on the plate sometimes affect a facsimile of Norman Mailer before the newfound woman of my life ("Can't you see that I love you!?" I bellow in my head, banging my fists on the table for exclamation) whisks away the plate, and with it our engagement, and demands payment for the fantasies I've just thrust upon her, and the food.

It's little more than that—bringing, conveying, shepherding the plate. "The perfect relationship," Johnny once described it, a line I've reiterated to X when, purposefully, willfully in the mood to consternate, I slyly let her know with my homage to his great quote, meant for posterity, that I was in love with my fat brother long before her skinny thighs.

And it *is* a perfect relationship. There's a taco counter in Bucktown who's over raw-onion-ing I've tired of, whose cook glances at me with a bit too much macho chest puff from behind the flattop, who will occasionally land a piece of grizzle amidst an otherwise enjoyable *birria* taco, thus ruining my day, but something keeps pulling me back to the corner carne-slinger, and she may not even be of age, but I have a sense she already has two kids, both of whom she'd leave behind, no doubt. Or, well, she can bring them. They'll forget Oscar or whomever, with the tattoo and too-rough way of teaching them about baseball. They'll take to me. They'll see how I'm gentler with their mother, how I let her speak and everything, how eager I am to improve my Spanish. Them, laughing at the *"pinche gordo gabacho,"* as we drive to the south side so she can show me her favorite place, past Pilsen, into Little Village, and she'll be nervous about her *abuela* not liking me, but, "No, no, no, *esta bien*," I'll reassure, and she'll giggle, uncertain. We'll go to said *abuela's* apartment, eventually, after consummation, after breaking her cherry on my homemade chorizo, and her *abuela* will have one of those multi-colored cowboy blankets over her lap, she'll be closer to four feet than five when she stands, and suspicious, more than a little mean. Until, that is, she sees the full Le Creuset I brought, and softens. Whenever the waitress looks at me, shyly, I see all this, and a smile almost wanting to play around the corner of her mouth, every time I'm there, which is usually on Saturdays. I know the schedule.

Ike has a different approach with the ladies—evident in the way he orders a pitcher, direct, subtly conspiratorial.

You know I could break anyone at this bar's face if you told me to, right? Anyone gets pervy, they'll be sorry, and walking funny tomorrow. Yep, just a pitcher, pronto, and I'm on your side, enforcing, not sexually-assaulting, forever.

It's a more indirect approach to Buffalo, more like the drifting-in of a late afternoon summer storm, where you forget the windows of the car are down before it's too late. He's blown in from the coast and his frame and bulky curling fingers are to be reckoned onto, into all plans, or almost all plans. Johnny will still spend the time between chicken wings strumming jazz chords, passing hours and member-when-ing with high school buddies on a comfy couch beside a bong in Allentown. Removing himself when necessary from overly-piled, too-small-house family time at Helka's. Ike will do the same, but the "assignment" has and will keep me at ground zero, Grandma's house, which is also where all three of us will end up tonight, and remain, until the tension snaps, until the hangover scrambled eggs and pancakes are rendered and the two of them go a couple preliminary rounds over bad coffee to feel out how the rest of the day, the trip, life, might go. We'll get back there, across Sheridan, for one-last-ones and a snack—that is, if we make it out of Caputi's un-arrested, intact, and still semi-familial.

The first pitcher always seems big, but it grows instantly feathery, wilty even, once Ike reveals his ace-in-the-hole, the son-from-far-away favor: Grandma is awaiting our call, to give us a lift home when finished. She will undoubtedly also drop much dough for the late-night cheesesteaks or tacos that we'll now have to prep ourselves, our guts, our gullets for.

"Shit, she shouldn't be driving at night," Johnny says, rarely the voice of reason but sobered by either a day's worth of bass player pot or his current company, who have a leg up on him, Ike and I having sauntered over after roast beef sandwiches, me having already nursed a whiskey and Ike two, three, maybe more deep.

"Fuck it, she's a big girl," Ike says, taking a swill, sizing us Rawski brothers up by the remnants in each of our pint glasses.

"Yeah, like 4'6." My moment for comedic relief, a chance, the clever but struggling poet character, the one everybody is rooting for in this movie. "We could walk," I add, taking Johnny's side.

"Walking's fine."

"Yeah. You 'member last time you walked home Teddy!?" Ike's voice rises and he gives me a beefy elbow nudge, eyes widening, shifting the pyramid base toward our end of the little round table. He's ribbing strategically, setting something up for later, and it's possible my character is now the over-analytical one that can't get a date, but not in the lovable way, in the aloof, malcontent one.

"Oh, shit, Ted told me this one," Johnny chimes in, back to life, shifting the dynamic again, changing sides.

"I told you, ok? I wanted to try the other Jim's." I hold up my hands in surrender, as if to say, *Whaddyawantfromme*?

"Yeah, the one in *North* Tonawanda!" Ike says, and with this comes a great collective guffaw, as if they'd never gotten lost for an hour or so on the six-some block cycle between Caputi's and Jim's and Helka's. "Hey Teddy. Hey Teddy," he goes on, rolling now, his eyes bleary from the last one-liner, "there ain't no Jim's in *North Tonawanda*." Johnny actually pounds the table with a fist as Ike's laugh gets to the uncontrollable animal state, it's almost a howl, and almost embarrassing to be at the center of.

Suddenly they feel all over me, like how well-coached, over-fed squirrels might attack, and I'm looking forward to telling Mom they seem to be getting along, sheepishly sipping, adjusting my hat, lifting it and putting it back on, scratching at my neck, enjoying family time and hoping for a commercial, maybe.

"Oh man, Johnny, are we gonna fuck him on the inheritance, eh?"

"Well, c'mon now, Ike. We'll buy him something. Maybe some beer!?"

"Yeah, one case, one case of Jenny Cream Ale!"

With this comes more wailing, cooing, high-pitched, teeth exposed, Ike having to finger the spittle out of his mustache and Johnny holding his belly. I nod in acceptance of my defeat, with a bit of capillary-burstage around the sideburn area. Sometimes it feels like a hockey game, and sometimes it feels like the ice is thin, or we're playing with our sticks curved the wrong way, or some kind of sports-as-life metaphor that a competent writer would know. A different kind of writer, the kind that knows how to end a night, or a sentence.

"You really on assignment?" Ike asks, downshifting, trying to fit the logistical workout time before the cross-eyed state we'll all enter on our way to the little house and couch-passing-out and snore-ignoring, seeming to eye me with some suspicion on this one, though it's hard to tell because I'm generally avoiding eye contact and hoping my bartender love doesn't look over while I'm being so vehemently jostled.

"Yeah, look at the research this one's doing!" Johnny reaches under the table in an effort to pat my gut through my hoodie.

"Yep. Research. See how many beers it takes Ike to proposition that fat guy over there with his hand-under-the-stall trick." I get it all back, the circle, the cycle, of life, fraternity rankings restored, pecking order challenged, something, and like that it's somebody else's turn to buy the next round.

"Teddy, I'll get this one," Ike says. "Can't count on Johnny."

"Yeah."

"Ya know, Teddy, whaddya call an unemployed jazz musician?" Ike thumbs a big digit Johnny's way, turning the tides. "Baroque!" The wails go up in threesome, hooting really, me pointing at Johnny as if to say "Bam, sucka!" Even though none of it makes sense, and a girls night out gathering nearby decides to move away from our table with subtle lip-raised snarls.

Much later, the last pitcher feels watery, and goes way too fast. Those often victim to "one more," that thing that necessitates bar time, an inability to remove your elbows from such comfy wood homes, from such in-the-pocket pulses, can easily fall down a black hole of regret around now. But by the time we're outside, me lighting three Camels at once in my mouth, passing one to each of my teammates, sucking deeply the smoke of crisp air cigarettes, there's a feeling of relief. No discussion of Dad, zero drunken orneriness, no O.J. talk, no throat-punching. Somehow, despite ghosts of adult judgment and decorum, Grandma is on her way to pick us up. So we smoke and point fingers and tilt our heads back to blow our lungs at the moon and imagine ourselves romantics of some sort.

It eventually happens, the Malibu inching up to the bar as if with a message, the non-Rawski smokers nervous, looking, everyone with an air of *who's this?*, the car crawling, then everyone seeing the diminutive gray-haired lady squinting, just tall enough to see over the wheel. Johnny rides shotgun and, after pointing Grandma towards Mighty, works some aux wire magic so that suddenly Al Green commandeers the car's tinny speakers, "I'm a Ram," the bass galoomphs and struts and thumps around the inside of the Malibu and the three drunk ones—*more* drunk, I should say, because Grandma's undoubtedly been sipping boxed wine while eyeing the clock, wondering, wanting her boys home and secure, not victim of the bad the late nights bring, always in the front of her mind—are rolling down windows and blowing smoke all around the north side of Buffalo.

"Grandma, whaddya think this song's about?" Johnny asks.

"Don't answer that, Ma," Ike warns. "He's goading you."

"Is it about driving?"

"Yeah, but into a woman." I say, straight-faced, back on it, feeling Al, who at the bar I said was my favorite singer of all time, firing up Ike and Johnny, allying them against me once again, before I'd footnoted my own observation with, "Well, or maybe Curtis." With this they both went hands-up-in-the-air, the frustrated *ahhs* laying claim over the whole barroom.

We're having serious discussion here.

-

And we're family.

-

And we don't give a fuuuuuuuck.

"Grandma, can you get back on the right side of the road," I say.

"Don't listen to him, Ma, he's goading you. Drive where you want."

"Ted, I've been driving for 65 years!"

"Time in the backseat with Grandpa doesn't count as driving!" Johnny with the step-back, for two.

"I don't know where we went wrong with these two." Ike says, all faux head-shaking and resignation.

It's less than a mile from Mighty to Helka's, and I'm out of the backseat before it feels the car is even stopped. By now I have almost no idea how we got home, how the arrangements were made, or how I ended up with a plastic bag full of beef and cheese burritos on my lap. A bag that is now becoming pointed at the ends, transfiguring itself, wrapping over with pigskin and laces before my glassy eyes, and now, either way, I'm miming. Out of the driveway, into the yard, it's me with the O.J. shoulder pads pumping like pistons, head high, surveying the playing field.

"Go man!" Ike shouts.

"Freddie Jackson!" Johnny yells. "Goooo!"

There's a memory in there somewhere, of the times, of at least once, from around four or five, when pure inertia and muscular leg churn was its own reward. When they got going themselves, the inward-pointing feet, faster and faster, snowballing, careening recklessly, full of virgin joy. But even if you look, and can find a semblance of a muscle recall, there are no adult times to remember what that bursting momentum feels like. Probably this is as close as you can get when you're almost 30 and you get that certain beery buzz of drunken family-piling happiness, where Grandma's your ride and there's no worry and the cigarettes in your pocket are enough for whatever the night brings and there's beer in the refrigerator and greasy ground beef wrapped in tortillas and love, to nurture you down into bed, the knowing it's there for a later comfort all that matters. Whiskey nostalgia brings back the rush of all the Bills blitzes, and the coursing collective adrenaline, and a we're gonna do it, god damn it, *we're gonna do it together, god damn Christ Freddie's gonna do it, OJ's going, Thurman's wide fucking open!* Back pats and open mouths and chairs and stools tipping and hitting the floor and nobody cares and high-fives becoming hugs. When you remember it all, at once, and the chasing of the past becomes an outright drunken bleed, it's so great that pure, stupid-grinned euphoria makes it so you should, yes, definitely, write down some of the evening's most profound revelations, discoveries, one-liner zingers. Or else, also, you should just run.

This is me. I can feel Helka shaking her head behind me, but Johnny and Ike are standing outside the car, one of them has his arms up in the touchdown stance, I'm sure, the other pumping his fist. I'm going full speed, and there's a nub of a tree, wooden remnants of oaken life in the middle of the yard. O.G. Johnny chopped it down on a summer afternoon of great musky, manly machismo, with his own hands, maybe *just* with his hands. It stands like a token of his *of course* victory over wildlife, and it's always been the baddest backyard defensive end this side of Bruce. Unmovable. Which is why you have to go over it.

Sweet mama's mashed potatoes, just don't drop the Mighty!

The blood is filling my ears, and I stutter-step to get the timing right. It's dark, with the grass wet, but the roar of the crowd, "SKIIIIIII!" is thunderous, and with all boozy abandon, a cigarette dangling from my lips, my left hand firmly out in stiff-arm position toward unseen linebackers, burritos firmly tucked in the other inner forearm like a ball, I plant, and leap, soaring through the dark unknown, over the long-dead tree.

14. CHICAGO (3-1)

People think of River North as success. Clean, white, sleek, sterile, close to a looming skyline, with new bars made to look old serving old cocktails made to look new, amid condo buildings erected with enticing long windows and names with umlauts. If you're here, you've made it. Rents are steep, but you can afford it because you went to a Big Ten school and studied Accounting or Management, and got slurry drunk most every night but didn't let Mommy and Daddy back in Dubuque down. Every girl on the street wears yoga pants while walking a tiny, ball-less dog, ball-less dogs that, luckily, you can pretend to look at while sizing up their owners' yoga-panted asses. Even for a cat man, the neighborhood is something.

Mostly repulsive, that something, and Dustin feels so, too, I can tell. Standing outside the restaurant, sucking on cigarettes in the darkening weekend night, trying not to do that thing that new friends in an out-of-context situation sometimes do—small talk. The filling in of details, like new work pals out at a bar on their first happy hour, or the first time a school chum comes to the house, meets Ma. Like we've already fucked, hard, passionate, too soon, and now you need to ask, awkwardly, if they have any siblings, if they have a job, if they, I don't know, like music.

We're not quite comfortable here, and it has nothing to do with Dustin or I, or our budding love, or his cool flat cap that makes him look like a Polish dockworker, arousing something approaching idolatry. Nor him telling me I could get a job "down by him," pay some bills, join the union, cheat on my timesheet, write on the side. "Hell, maybe you could even teach me a thing about writing," he says, from way down in his gut, but with the register going up at the end, gaining assurance, delivered with such *basso profundo* certainty. No doubt, all childhood fear forgotten, even when he's laughing at himself, ourselves, or the Bills.

"Dustin, I would like nothing more than to tell you all my thoughts, hopes and theories on writing. Whilst drinking all night." I blow a ponderous plume of smoke out the corner of my mouth and watch a new mom maneuver a stroller down Chicago Avenue.

"That's what I'm saying! *Whilst!*"

We *har-har* and guffaw, Dustin slapping his thigh, and he's pulling a second cigarette out of his pack. I follow suit, neither of us wanting to go back in, not yet, not with our fiancés hitting it off like fiancés do over margaritas at a fancy-ish, trendy French-inspired Tex-Mex joint that bellows about its duck having been *confit*-ed.

Double-header cigarettes never taste quite right, not unless they come after two hasty Don Julio shots and happen along newfound love. This one tastes fine, I guess, and I feel the night going somewhere, maybe even toward dropping the ladies off at our respective pads, or leaving them at some swanky corner spot we can trust, where they can share Carrie Bradshaw-esque girl intimacies about tampons and eye-rolls about toilet seats being left up and penis size, wide-eyed *oh reallys* over Dustin's penchant for wanting to have sex through the pee hole of his Bills pajama bottoms. The usual feminine talk always takes place over chocolatinis in my mind, with a doting gay bartender keeping the creeps away and making sure everything's ok, lubed and jovial and jocular—despite good natured ribbings about their future husbands, of course. They laugh together over our mannish doltishness, they themselves sophisticated, part of some elite martini-glass-wielding Masons-for-the-feminist-age society. Meanwhile, Dustin and I will be pounding Maker's at Richard's, smoking and carelessly ashing into Styrofoam coffee cups provided by a bartender who stands with one knee up and towel over his shoulder, a disinterested, faraway look in his eyes. We'll figure out everything wrong with the Bills blitz package and get bleary-eyed and back-patting into the honest hours.

How we got roped into a double date isn't easy to work out. Truthfully, it was as much my percolation for Dustin as it was for someone else—*anyone else*—to take the burden off of X and I's conversations of late. Rents versus condos, mostly, confounded by the secret that I still don't know what a condo is. Then there's the fact that just the other morning, as I bent to tie my Nikes for yet another belabored trip out with the business-suited Asian woman who has now become a part of our little cluster of people we have to deal with on a normal basis, I noticed her noticing the thinning lightness on the top of my head. Sexual interest seemed to wane, go chilly, that and subsequent nights. There was a look approaching confusion I thought I'd never seen before, as if she was just noticing something, as if she were just noting my sideburns with new scrutiny, with squinty eyes, like you might go over a tiny nick in your windshield.

But now we're back at the table, and I'm self-consciously finger-stroking my splotchy facial hair and patting the top of my dome. The conversation seems not to have changed since Dustin boldly proclaimed, "Smoke time!" Actually, it seems not to have changed since last September, or was it the one before?

"We're looking to buy, maybe," X says, giving me that look, the one I've gotten since four years ago, when people would start throwing the "R" or "E" word around. The *step up your game* look, the sense of *it's time for adulthood* and *you sissy little mama's boy bitch, buy a ring already, get engaged.*

"Pilsen. Maybe Little Village." I try to flag the waitress, who probably doesn't live around here but, from the pants, looks like she could.

"Teddy! No! No, we're not, just cuz of that taco place you love." X cackles oddly, apologizing to the table for my ribeye problem.

"Further south, then."

"Teddy!" She swills, out of desperation, like Dustin does with his home-brought beer bottles during review timeouts that are obviously being reversed against Buffalo. It's the universal antidote to reality, even for X. Apparently I've found little that is truly my own in nascent adulthood, though that doesn't stop me from furiously trying to flag the waitress.

If we were home and she were sober, this defiance would inspire a death gaze, but she's three deep and in performance mode, so we like each other, and, as though one of us were looking for another term, are repeatedly letting our constituents know.

Haha, jokester, that Teddy, ohhh, so amusing, drink up, table. Here, I'll start.

"Well, don't blow all your savings on a place. Don't forget that little matter of the Jim Kelly jersey you promised me!" Dustin says, and guffaws heartily, making genuine eyes at his betrothed, a number upon meeting and shaking hands with I sized up as Tuesday morning. Midwest fair and plain, friendly, your standard draw play on 1st-and-10 after a touchback. But upon this, and her lighten-and-grin at Dustin, there's a familiar way that hints they've discussed this topic before, talked about *me*, maybe after that first game, and the sacks and the beatdown and how he got a bit sheepish and asked for my number, and I find myself warming to her.

With this, the invocation of greatness, a settling of rising tension, there's a détente, even the waitress appears by my side, and all lights are green before us, allowing a return to stasis, to Dustin's low-end decree of humor, humility, and timely Bills-remembering.

But then it comes: girlish margarita-soaked piquedness, X's voice sounding like it probably did in 10th grade when her dad handed her the phone and it was a handsome tennis player, or rock bassist, or one of those nebulous bad boys who had a bit of facial hair too early and a skateboard, and she was suddenly trying too hard, unable to control her adolescent voice coming out so squeaky, peakish, and even the waitress, patiently awaiting which type of mescal I'll have, can sense the *faux pas*, her eyebrows raising too upon the sacrilege.

"Who's Jim Kelly again?" X asks.

It hits like a blasphemy littered with N-words on a quiet bus spewed in chorus by random Midwestern grandmothers, the gang of them simultaneously screaming at the top of their lungs, then running amok down the street, through the restaurant, with knives in their teeth, adorned in tattered nightgowns. It's like the worst dick joke, leveled at full volume, just when the music fades. It is a fart during sex. An extended doggystyle scene during movie viewing with Mom, while you're visiting her in the hospital.

What else could cause Dustin—a man bordering on Tourette's, the giddy kind, unable to help himself from such outbursts as "Make a sports play!" during the slow segue into coverage after commercial timeouts—to be unable to even *look*? His fiancé, whose name I've forgotten, who I've fallen in love with, who I don't want to see this, my lowest of many low moments, even she knows the level of trespass, being as she is, and given her relationship. She takes one of those nervous sips of water, offers an unsure smile, and gives a head nod toward X as if to say, "Let's powder our noses."

And that's it, the dream pulverized, smashed like the mint in my forthcoming post-dinner mojito by so many bearded, burly bartenders. I can see myself and the entire audience, their collective *awww*, hearts breaking, for me, and all my future bride misunderstands. I'm suddenly, in this crucial moment, either at Delilah's, by myself, over a rocks glass, head in hand, a disinterested but sympathetic bartender polishing glasses, holding each up to the light, ignoring me, or otherwise I'm standing over the river, gazing up at the Hancock at twilight, the hulking beauty of my adopted city rending me aptly miniscule, withered, destroyable.

X has the confit, of course. Enjoys every bite, in a weird oblivion of *oohing* and *ahhing* and condos and rings and engagements and deadlines and plans and business casual and adult time that cause me to keep drying my palms on my pants thighs. I float thoughtlessly through too-chocolatey mole and bites I would normally find inoffensive, filling, possibly even enjoyable, but simply scarfing now, leaning, so that I can make evident it's time for Dustin to announce "Smoke time!" once again and we can stand and I can unstick my boxers from my butt cheeks discreetly amongst peers who know how to iron shirts before going to such a restaurant on such a weekend night, where we're all supposed to make it count.

Dustin's a shipper and receiver, but that's not how he says it. Not shipper *and* receiver, but like it's one word, *shipperreceiver*. Emphasis lands on both *ers*, indicating stuff being done to other stuff. Action things, progress. Taking care of business, world commerce. People tired at the ends of days, ties loosened, sleeves pushed up on dress shirts that fit. Not Dustin, though, he's all about the butt end of the economy, the sweaty side of hourliness, veiny forearms and taking showers after work.

Yes, the smoke time talk has come back to the small kind, but amidst loose plans with myself, congealing like the mole, to keep my place, Dustin is genuinely offering to show me around, to let me, "Wrap a few pallets. *Man work*," the latter delivered in an even lower voice, one used to distinguish, entice, persuade. He does me a favor and pretends it has nothing to do with the fact that my life has begun to untangle one seam at a time.

"Yeah man, just until you sell the book."

"And teach you about writing."

"Of course. *And teach me about writing!*"

We smoke and laugh and look at what's becoming a club-going crowd—heels too high and tight blackness all over, products of an expensive kind congealing hair into place, lips brightened, tits popping in impossible ways at 90-ish degree angles, eyes ahead, not set on the tall and fat-ish guys patting their guts and sucking Camels, but on making it to a definitive destination with a name like Silke or Envey, seductively misspelled, or so some big-dick developer who probably knows our Asian friend well once thought.

"I'm sorry about the Kelly thing," I finally say, not looking, kicking at a tumbleweed in my head, feeling far from God and home and Buffalo and Johnny and Ike and even Grandma.

"What Kelly thing?" Dustin smirks, still bellowing somehow though his voice is low and conspiratorial.

"I fucked up here, and I want to be better. Listen, we don't have to go back in. I know a place around the corner..." I hope the pleading isn't as obvious in the dark, wishing the puppy dog-ishness out.

"Next time, man. Next time."

"Next time."

"And shit, man, listen, about the Kelly thing... I've heard *worse* jokes."

We both know it's not true, though, and as we saunter back in toward nightcaps and whatever it is nightcaps put on to go to sleep, ahead of maybe *just one more* on the way home, we don't laugh at all.

15. FAMILY TREE
4346 N. Bailey Ave.
Buffalo, NY 14226

I picture Proust here. He'd have to be, what, in his 190s by now? And I picture Teressa, too—chicken wings were actually never really her thing.

Enough with the spice and the red sauce blotting up her clean counters, splotching about the white stovetop, necessitating so much 409, stinking the air to high heavens (there are no heavens but the "high heavens" with these types of women, no "low heavens" or even "middle heavens"). Always with that piercing vinegar-ness, to say nothing of her apron, or bowels. You can't breathe after a while, the grease coats your skin, everything feels sheeny, like it's just been wiped with a wet nap, and then another wet nap is the only way to get said sheen off. It gets under her poor fingernails, the cuticles scarred irreparably by the zing of Frank's Red Hot. Teressa has always secretly rued the day she invented those fandangled (everything is "fandangled" with women of this age, too) tips of poultry, and invited into her humble family watering hole the magnitudes of rotund alkies with their stained sweatshirts and too-guttural *howyadoins*, the constant sucking on the tips of their fingers and their order for 'nother rounds before even being done with their current sweating Molsons, which get no respect save for a greedy deep-throating and clack back on the bar. What would the ladies from church think, for Christ's sake? And don't forget Christ! She hasn't taken a solid, non-spicy shit in years.

What's wrong with who she used to be? she often wonders, slicing through another amalgamation of tendon and skin to separate the wings. She would gaze off wistfully, were she not so in fear of the very real threat of a knife slip and digit dismemberment. *Focus, Teressa, focus!* She can almost always hear them from the front, drunkenly wanting *'nother* something. Still, without gazing, she remembers the old, simpler days, when she could enjoy bad, watery cups of tea served in puce cups on paper placemats, in joints with neon signs and a nice old, fat Greek gentleman with a toothpick in his mouth who always greets you by name when you walk in, and who, upon being seated, you must always comment upon, "Oh, *that's* the *owner*, such a nice man." Never mind the undocumented Mexican sweeping the floor for peanuts, or maybe bits of feta, and the fact the obviously well-fed owner gets a new Cadillac *every year*, one he parks in an awkward manner in front of the door where there should probably be a handicap spot.

Here we have the Family Tree, a joint where you can and should go during the day. In fact, this may be *the* joint, seeing as how they probably invented the early bird dinner. The coffee is always on, and always burnt, even if it just got done brewing, and behind every waitress' smile is a sad heart and broken story. One too many kids, or one too few; one too many years in Vegas, or she never left for California; the one that got away, or the one perpetually handsy, whom she could never leave. So you tip big, don't make fun of the comically-applied eyeliner, and never complain about the coffee.

Proust could indeed be happy in a corner booth, joining Teressa, overlooking Bailey and the neighboring Liquor Box, a bodega that has contributed so much liver failure to the Rawski family tree. How the word torrents might rush forth from the writer at this diner closest to my childhood home. This fact would hold some kind of significance to him, some kind of filial gravity, and he would gush, analyze like Freud, about the latency of my chicken erections, and my feta cheese obsession signifying Mommy issues, and my diners-are-the-best-place-to-eat claim from some barely publishable story I wrote one time.

Then he'd go on, on a tangent of his own, pondering the raisins in the rice pudding, but, unlike with the peaches, or whatever sent him on that infamous rant in a time when editors were more generous, here he'd have a point, the way the raisins secretly populate underneath the whip cream layer. Like an apartment building, so sleepy on the outside, and then you go through the front door and there's the swirl and boom of a million little lives swimming about—their garbage, their locked bikes, their mailboxes with free menus sticking out, everything colliding in a soupy stew that wafts thick, like the smell of Indian food. They burst in your mouth, those raisins, and every time you order, the waitress has to clarify, "You want raisins in that?" It's the equivalent of her asking, pausing from scratching her scalp or ass with the pen, which she's always doing, "Do you hate Hitler?"

"All my family wants to do is eat chicken wings," Teressa says, to Proust, slurping tea, easing toward comfort, the grease drying on her face in this distance from her kitchen.

"The souvlaki here, though, it's sublime, exquisite, the way the ember harkens obsequiously…"

Helka's here, too, in the same booth. She dropped by, driving the Malibu herself, doing her old lady saunter through the parking lot, her feet barely off the ground and a slight hobble, her little purse full of crisp 20s dangling from a 90-degree forearm. Inside, she stops every now and again to catch her breath, and the waitress scoots by on her way to refill some bad coffee with hotter burnt coffee. Helka spotted the other early birders and figured *what the hell*, I'll give them a piece of my mind, and now she's interrupting Proust, doing everyone a favor.

"Teddy says this place is haunted. Or, no, not haunted, *jizzed* on. Or, no, that's not right. The jibes, something with the jibes?"

"Vibes. I had vibes once…" Proust says, thinking about taking off, maybe flying.

"He thinks Jim couldn't find his helmet because of this place."

"Ya lost me, Helka."

"Jim. *Kelly*? Are you listening, Marcel!? Teressa, you believe this guy?

103

He couldn't find his helmet after halftime, missed a drive, and the Bills lost."

"Are you sure it was...?"

"I'm sure. Teddy's life, Johnny's life, ruined. Fucking losers the both of them, truth be told."

"Your judgments..." Proust tries to stick up for me and Johnny, and it should be a great moment, us together on this quest of truth and over-pontificating, brothers with forks.

"Fuck 'em," Helka cuts him off. "Both of 'em. Fuck Ohio, and Chicago's even worse. Dickheads ain't even got time to call anymore. Not that I care, I stopped caring, it's just..."

"Fuck 'em?"

"Fuck 'em. That's right. Thank you, Teressa."

You want to come about 4 or 4:30 on any weekday afternoon, to munch chicken souvlaki, rice pudding, and, if you're like me, imagine coffee-cup conversations between your grandmother and Marcel Proust that trample leftover Super Bowl ghosts. The vibes still stink, sunken as they are like cigarette smoke, which is also still sunk around the purplish, plastic-y booths, reminders of the good old days, when my dad sat with a big beard and glasses and nursed hangovers with Marlboros while Teddy chowed Mickey Mouse pancakes and Johnny wouldn't shut his mouth about something Eric Clapton played, or Stratocasters, wearing a Pink Floyd t-shirt two sizes too big and little-kid carrying on about some such business and his idiotic dreams while Dad rubbed his temples.

Antiquity, family history, and an undeniable bit of Greek brilliance. It might start with the table dressing, a massive corked vase of Greek oil, one that O.G. Johnny likened to Mississippi Mud. Even doing so on the day of Super Bowl 25, joking, though he was nervous, noticeably so, shaken a bit, the excitement down, the fidgeting up, even a prepubescent Teddy finding the need to wipe his palms with the realization that everything before, all the fun and the beatdowns, the clamors of "Bruuuuuce," the desperate cries of "blitz," would be for nothing if we blew it. A waste. To work and struggle a whole life and not get published, to make all the sauce and overcook the wings.

To whomp Miami and run roughshod—O.J. style—over a flim-flam AFC of the early-90s, for the first of many times, to be the biggest dick at the porn star convention, to have a well-earned bullseye square on the ass, to face the fear of failure, like a champion, and...

And then to not center the ball, to rush Scotty and his poor little facemask—couldn't they get the guy a decent facemask?—and to give it all away.

Welcome to the majors, kid. Kids, actually, for it wasn't but one life ruined that day by Family Tree and her tender, perfect souvlaki chicken cubes, her good food and bad vibes, and Scott Norwood missing a kick.

"It sounds like your family is just like mine, Helka," Teressa says, taking a swill of the hot stuff, preparing herself and that sensitive old lady appetite, the kind that craves leafy greens doused in the muddy table dressing.

"Yeah. Bunch o' fucking wing-stinking losers," Helka says, smiling and waving to the owner back behind the counter.

"Whaddya wanna get married for, anyway?" Johnny asks, legitimately confused. "Fuck it all up. Fuck everything up."

"I'm not like you fucks. I have a heart."

"You got so much heart?" Ike asks, incredulous. "I didn't even see you crying after Super Bowl 28."

"Again with the *Teddy didn't cry*. I been hearing that my whole goddamn life!"

My hands are up, exasperated, face a bit flushed. Didn't I cry? Didn't I bleed? Were my wrists not open and gushing with the liquid equivalent of everything that could have been? Have I not been paying these past 20-some years for caring *too much*? Have I not pondered late into boozy nights and woozy daydreams, on rooftops in Chicago and all-night bars in New Orleans, in ladies' beds and on my mother's couch, atop the shitter and in a pew, from late-night walk-through drive-thrus at Mighty Taco to predawn frijoles in Pilsen, from please-don't-call-on-me grade school to I'm-too-stoned-to-actively-contribute-to-this-classroom-discussion-so-please-don't-call-on-me college? How different it could have been, how much better, had I not followed the contrarians next door and just rooted for the Cowboys.

"Why didn't you cry, Teddy?" Johnny asks, backing up Ike.

The two of them in unison, almost goading me, yes, certainly that, but Ike and Johnny both have that quizzical eyebrow scrunch thing about them and the deadpan *How* so emphasized that makes a person with any conscience or desire to assimilate in decent common humanity backpedal. Question his own heart, his devotion, his love. If I'm not moved enough by the crippling throat punch (Super Bowl 25), kidney shot (Super Bowl 26), ensuing inability to perform (everyone gets where this is going), and "of course this would happen to me" blue balls (the day, the game, the dividing point of life, in question), to gush moisture from eye crevices, to weep uncontrollably, inconsolably, to lose all emotive shit and governance, how do I know enough to get married? To commit? Who's to say I've ever been invested? Do I actually, in fact, care? Where is the blood spilled, the loyalty, the band of brotherhood? The jumping on top of landmines? Have we ever gone down in a plane together? Pricked fingers with non-cauterized safety pins and swapped plasma in the Magic Johnson-era of AIDS? Crossed enemy forests? Risked Amazonian crocodile swamps with nothing but a charging Buffalo on our hats and the collective *belief* in our hearts?

"I cried after that preseason game last year, remember?"

"Ah fuck, Teddy." Ike dismisses with both palms, waving with arms outstretched, casting me off as another front-runner. Johnny just smiles.

The thing is, I can't recall Ike crying. Nobody can. He was gone. "Fishing," as O.G. Johnny put it. A head pat of an excuse, a "go play while the grownups talk" statement of Ike's need for West Coast re-location, the sudden sweeping of his usual dinner time position out of our lives. Sparing me, mostly, from the instructions Johnny got:

"Anybody calls, asks you anything, you don't know where he is."

"But we *don't* know where he is," I said once, a precocious tiny bastard overhearing something not intended for his inward-pointing feet and mop top and sniveling questions he didn't know enough not to ask.

"That's right," O.G. Johnny replied, beaming down at me from behind the ubiquitous mustache. Always beaming, anytime that I reminded him of my presence beneath his Herculean stature. A physique full of shoulders, more than two, surely, wide and ex-panding, a Clark Gable wispiness to the hair but all callousses and ruddiness on his fingers, meant for fighting Nazis, for working with lumber and super glue and hammers in the sawdust-smelling basement, meant for sliding through the little nook nub of an old mug with a globe stretching around its curvature, sipping Helka's bad coffee. Fingers also meant for hexing opposing quarterbacks, his move part Western New York voodoo and a touch of Polish Santeria, from back in the old country: on third-and-long, or anytime a QB unlucky enough to have to run a shotgun set on the opposite side of Bruce Smith would line up, O.G. would lead Johnny and I, maestro-like, in extending arms and fingers of both hands toward the TV, and ruthlessly, repeatedly, in trance-like exasperation, chant the words *whammy, whammy, whammy.*

O.G. was all satiny Grandpa pants and impossibly soft buttondowns. He was also straight brim baseball hats long before and apart from that look becoming cool, becoming *street.* He seemed mildly street though, actually, from behind the wheel of the new-every-three-years but no-electric-windows Buick. Windbreaker fresh, pants pressed, hands at 10 and 2, but an insouciance about it, a badassery that belied his Grandpa-ness, the pants and the moth balls and Old Spice and Stetson and flabbiness under the arms and ignorance as to Led Zeppelin, but 97 Rock on regardless, for our benefit. The old man still went to church every Sunday, to keep Helka happy, and the way he drove, slow, sure through turns and obnoxiously deliberate blind spot checks, was like how your uncle is always cooler than your dad, even when he's doing the same thing in the same way. The sense of awe it instills, the wonder at DNA, the feel of knowing which one you want to become.

He carried it that way up to the end. The shoulders withered a bit those last days in the hospital, sure, but that could have also been the perspective from my own suddenly expanding college beer gut.

"You taking up space in college?" he asked from the hospital bed.

"No, Grandpa, you got the joke wrong!" Back from college, with the long hair it inspired, I sat there with him, unsure, out of place in what was supposed to be a time of gravity, of seriousness. *How's your hippie idealism serve you now?* the sanitary white corridors of death seemed to ask. Amid the reeking disinfectant, everything I'd sought to project—love, pacifism, that I know where to score pot and like to party—seemed impossibly farther away than Chicago and the short flight.

Not as far, though, as a time when Grandpa was steering with those big paws, up across Sheridan, "We're gonna stop at the *gin mill,*" his old refrain. I was little, in the back seat, and he'd turn with the half-smirk to Johnny and I. And so maybe Grandpa's to blame? For the draconian hurt my brother and I have placed on count-less gin mills from NYC to SF, from Milwaukee to Baton Rouge, from mid-afternoon to half-past bar time, just trying to follow and find that big man behind the wheel. The mythological essence he breathed into it—*gin mill*—a place of lost dreamers, bleary smil-ing poets, blue-collar end-of-day rewards. What we deserved. The way it rolled off the tongue, hinting at refreshment and evening renewal, sanctuary from wind and all those words that end in *-ing,* communal nocturnal rebirth set to the theme of *Cheers.*

"Don't be ridiculous, she knows who Jim Kelly is."

I'm not sure who says it, but I've been punted out of my revelry and put back on D. Like a sack by Bruce, like a Polska pierogi of wicked juju boomeranging back toward me from decades before, *whammy, whammy, whammy.*

Although the Bills are getting throttled—O.G. Johnny's picture turned to the wall since two minutes left in the first quarter, when Fitz, ditzing on uniform color or something, mistaking Miami white for the referee, perhaps, or failing to see the Ike-like monstrosity shadowing him from ten feet away, staring him down, flitzed a wounded daffodil over the middle which was returned for a touch-down like an overcooked steak sent back by any Robert DeNiro character—Ike and Johnny seem to be picking up beer can steam.

Like O.J. with a blocker, in those big pads, rumbling like a juiced up gazelle alongside a slightly fatter gazelle, always finding downhill on a flat playing surface. Helka's puttering around in the kitchen, still in slippers, measuring the chunks of Velveeta, wondering if it'll be enough for the rest of the stay, the rest of the day, but also just hiding out, afraid of the big ones, rumbling, frightened for her little Teddy, who's about to get tag-teamed by a gaggle of sauced rapscallions.

Especially at this point in modern Bills-watching history, at this point in time, too, after I've put on 14 pounds in 30 days of Buffalo-living, after I've out pizza-eaten Ike one Tuesday near bar time at Caputi's, where nobody was left but the fat Rawskis giddily chiding each other about how many pieces of pepperoni constitute a "real slice," after I've become acquainted and re-acquainted with all of the new high school girls that operate the walk-through at Mighty Taco, after the Bills have Buffaloed the season, and the heart of everyone, one hoof and then another, an endless angry hoofing from a million-pound mammal, the flavor of camaraderie takes on a different tone. At 0-1, there's hope, at 5-5 there's *maybe*, at 5-6 there's little but spite, fizzing like a dropped can of ginger ale, chippy and beleaguered, much scoff and scowl. It's now that the absurdity of life shows itself in a Fitz misread. In a lofted third down pass that never had a chance. Everybody is covered, and it's the point in the season where you know ahead of time, before the snap, like opening the refrigerator for a look-see when you distinctly remember having already finished the last beer.

How different it might have been, had Johnny and I been a generation earlier, of the bar crowd in the glory days. To have been down at the gin mill instead of waiting for Helka to bring more Hormel pepperoni slices and melt some cheese-like substance, any will do, over something salty, whatever is fine, and bring it to the TV trays resting under each of our outstretched arms.

How different we'd all be now, had the kick not wide-righted. Johnny would most likely be of the polo shirt varietal, on the other end of his country club affairs, not playing so many notes, such fancy chords, to compensate. Meanwhile my hair would be combed, I'd have hair, maybe even a part. Possibly a nice bottle of shampoo, the good stuff, Swedish name, so good that on commercials they need to zoom in and get a cartoon reenactment of all the serious cleansing going on at the cellular level. That gut would have been aborted before I even thought of my first half-marathon, or 50K, something done and photographed for social media, smiles and athletic shorts and victory over life before a huge lunch with peers and adoring kids and frothy mugs, well-deserved. I'd scoff at cigarette ads, and eat Mighty but once a week. I'd still live here, in Buffalo, hometown proud, with a barber and regular diet and a condo, such as it would go after tasting the nectar of mainstream positive reinforcement.

Instead, in Chicago, it would be desperate laughs and pleading Dustin shouts. Simple, guttural, "Make a sports play!" The early winter drinking fraught, pathetic, but at least the anxiety would be gone, the pressure released. An ease in the flow of palm sweat. We'd toast and clink High Life bottles over the Camus of it all, laugh existentially, though combined we've never read one of his books, or even a page. A field goal attempt down 24-3, an interception down two scores with 30 seconds left, a really sweet, booming *varoomph* of a punt. These get-togethers, once for the game, could begin to resemble support groups. Us vs. them, the 'them' being the gods, all pertinent contributors to the league, society.

Back here, though, in Buffalo, the smell of blood seems about the air, like something Mexican grandmothers get up early to make, and let simmer all day. I can't tell if they are picking on me, or X, or both. Or each other, somehow. Possibly even poor, puttering Helka. My cat seems in the line of fire, too, such is the pervasive something-dead-in-the-wall stink line of rancor.

"Ehhh...Teddy..." Ike starts.

"I don't know why I told you guys that. Fuck. She was drunk, alright?"

"Being drunk is an excuse for lots of things," Johnny chimes in.

"Like you being born."

"Tequila drunk, ok?"

"Teddy," Ike, leans forward, points square at my chest. "You are fucking kidding yourself."

"And she had just gotten concussed." The words are spewing out in self-defense.

"I'm embarrassed for you."

"No, really, she was in this bar fight..."

Johnny laughs. "Oh, Teddy, what are you, Fitz on third down!?" He's miming a panicked quarterback, patting the ball, looking to, fro, desperate.

"But really, how are you gonna fit a ring over your sausage finger?" Johnny sits back, not even looking my way, raising a slice over his mouth, letting the front cheese dangle, hover, methodically enter his mouth before the tip of the brilliant pizza triangle, spit pockets glistening at the corners of lips.

"Hey-ohh!" Ike likes this enough to get off his seat, simultaneously high-fiving Johnny and finishing the dregs of a can of Genesee.

I pretend to focus on the game, but it's a commercial, a shampoo commercial. I almost want to get out, there's almost a feeling I've maybe never had before, of wanting some air, some space between this and the last interception I only half-saw.

"I'm gonna take a nap—I mean *walk*, I'm gonna take a walk." It's a Freudian slip, or something, the word *take* generally only preceding *nap* or *dump*.

"Why don't you walk your ass to the fridge to get me another beer?" Ike says, cold, accusatory, disappointed, a bit distant.

"Who wants pepperoni?" Helka asks from the doorway, pleading with her eyes for something to do, for someone to feed, for a back to scratch, for a steaming mug to pour in defense of encroaching winter.

"Bad timing, Ma. Teddy don't wanna talk about sausage."

Whammy, whammy.

Even the pizza seems abused, cheapened, but I walk to the kitchen for another slice. Actually I stop on the way from the getting of requested beers, and Helka is there again, at the kitchen table, cup before her on the plastic-y tablecloth. She's back in her nightgown, in retreat, staring out the window.

"Ah, Grandma, come on. They're just ribbing me."

"Oh, Teddy, I know. It's not that."

"She didn't get in a bar fight, either!" I grab a slice, grinning, hearing Johnny in the next room, *"and then I says, you're like Fitz!"* and the two of them in back-of-the-class stitches.

"No, Teddy, no."

"What then? The Bills? You should be used to it." I bite into the slice without bothering to sit, taking a second bite with my mouth still full.

"Teddy."

"And you know I cried." I pick pepperoni off the rest of the pie, adding one to my own slice and popping another in my mouth.

"How could you marry someone…"

"She's half-Catholic, I told you!" Arms out in a *whaddyawant* query, I segue easily into a crucified J.C. display`.

"… that doesn't know who Jim Kelly is?"

With this the Grandma tears burst forth, and my chewing stops, and the laughter, there all along, waiting for Grandma's unintentional punchline, comes booming, carrying on like the Niagara, cascading from the living room, at my expense.

17. CHICAGO (4-1)

Since Smoke left, it's just me and the cat, and the little guy never cares how long I hog the toilet. Sometimes, especially of late, I even let my furry friend in, to watch, to sit on the edge of the tub and maybe get inspired for a more sensible approach to the whole dumping procedure. For him to see it done like a man, an adult, with cleanliness and hygiene and two-ply and the vent turned on and the faucet, too, for an extra white noise barrier between anyone unfortunate enough to be within earshot on the other side of the apartment door. To see how to conduct your private matters with dignity, and discretion. This also offers me a chance to affect some condescension, "See how I don't *lick my own asshole* when I'm done?"

Doing it all, playing at professionalism, adulthood, despite the no-longer-imminent risk of the roommate bounding through the rickety wooden front door, always so pronounced in its low-rent ricketiness, tramping down the hallway toward his bedroom until he spots the closed door, hears the faucet, and unable to stop himself, bellows, "*Dumping* time! Eh, Ski!?" and knocks the door with one single punch, for emphasis, for announcement.

"Getting it warm for you," I'd say upon hearing him, letting his presence change atmospheric matters, for my mind and for my colon, for whatever reading material was at hand and the cup of coffee I like to have nearby, cooling, within reach, by the sink.

"Don't whole-hog it, dog!" he'd shout, *whole-hog* a Smoke colloquialism for many fat guy things: grabbing the last slice of pizza without the societal, polite *you done?*; snagging the last bottle from a roommate's six-pack of good stuff; eating your third jalapeno popper from a shared order of five without offering to cut the last one in half. In this through-the-closed-door instance, though, he would be instructing me to not sit too far back, to not encompass the entire circumference of the toilet seat with my ass, as if it were somehow less gross if I reserved some cool porcelain for his own person, should he want to use it immediately after, which he far too often did.

But Smoke's tiny bedroom, just next door, now sits empty, save for some dust bunnies and a few tape marks where there used to be posters. His key still rests where he left it on the counter, me unable to look, to think about it or the four-ish years we had here. His couch is gone from the living room, as is most of the cookware. And the coffee table. And his pot, and those last three Goose Islands I was counting on for nostalgic time, to sip on after he'd bent and picked up the last box, as the standard scene played...

"So, yeah, if you change your mind, ya know, I won't have the lock changed and...dammit, Smoke, we've been through so much, and you can always come home. I want you to know that. I need you to know that."

"Huh?" He's already down the hall, out of earshot, affecting the annoyed manner people with awkward boxes in front of them have, all shifting and lifting with alternating knees, frustrated.

"It's just that, I want to tell you..."

"Ski! What!? What the fuck? I can't hear you, can you just get the door, man?"

"Oh, yeah, right...sorry." I hustle down the hall, hiding the tears, and he avoids eye contact, moving through the door. "It's just..."

"Yeah?"

"Fine."

"Huh?"

"It's fine. Just go. Did you take all the beers?"

He doesn't answer, already sliding through the elevator door, propping his last box and the last vestige of our domesticated bliss against the wall inside. Out of my life, our life, forever. Or until next weekend, when he realizes the mistake he's made and wants to come over for a Friday night bong and beers and *Graceland* session. This is all I want to tell him, but I'm left holding open the door, mouth agape, jilted, empty-nested.

Since he left, I've been on the love seat, eating frozen pizzas on their own cardboard, resting said pies on my lap, keeping the hot sauce and scrunched paper towel in hand, beer on the floor by my feet, ash tray precariously perched on the armrest. Much time has been spent pondering rent, thinking on writing, wondering how many calorie-scribing assignments it'd take to venture a solo life, staring blankly toward the wall, wondering, *what next*? Even more time has been spent sitting on the toilet, as I am now, unrushed, dangerously unperturbed, a tingling entering my thighs. Vent on, out of habit, and faucet running, like that whole thing from Siddhartha, lending soothing rivulets for meditation time.

I think of changes, minor edits, thematic shifts. I ponder, as I often do, the great burden of my literary philosophy: namely, how it is that no great book character ever takes a shit? Now, from this perch, it is clear. This is the thing, the linchpin to selling the manuscript. A perfect chapter, it just needs some lube, and to be inserted immediately, right in the middle of the epic but clearly too-short novel. A ten-page entry whose entire flourish tangles within the space and possibility of a single midday bowel movement, just like now, with our hero seated, as per usual. Think of what it all means, to retreat, to step back behind the door of society and her fully-clothed pleasantries. The calm, and subsequent recalibration. A readjustment of the boxers and pants, a thorough hand washing, a splash of cool water on the face. What better time for literary epiphany? The swirling, the release, the refresh, courtesy of two surging gallons of Lake Michigan water.

At the very least such new writerly inspiration gives a real reason to continue holding off on calling back X, to let the silent treatment run for a bit longer, before the unnecessary discomfort required to extinguish that particular fire, "Forget it" never meaning *forget it*, this just the beginning, no forgetting will be done before ten rounds and a never-unanimous decision.

Forget it.

Alrighty. Wanna smoke some pot and watch the Comeback Game?

Yeah! (Whole-heartedly, enthusiastically, getting a wet clitoris and such.)

It's childish, this no-speaking game, and even Dustin could see it was childish, laughing it off by the end of the night, pounding post-dinner mojitos and slapping me on the back with every one of my backup offensive lineman name remembrances from the Bills glory days—this a game we like to keep going when it gets late enough, when the nostalgic wheels are adequately slick. Though he, like me, still wanted to punch something, to break something, to squash the ignorance, the disbelief, with a great grab-and-shake of her shoulders, rocketing her head around on her neck, maybe even with a hearty wake-up slap for exclamation, all the time yelling, "Whaaaat!? Four straight Super Bowwwwls!"

He would remind me later, when things settled down—after the ladies had split a cab toward our respective pads, me not offering to give X the key to my place, her knowing I was upset but not showing it, still in "company" mode, banking this slight in the armory for a future fight—when we were head down over a bar far away from River North, amidst Dustin's grounds in the Village, when he had said it stolidly, poetically, "Ski, you don't know who her favorite quarterback is." And he laughed, while I grinned.

"Whoever it was, is, he was no fucking Jimbo." I raised my glass for a profound cheers.

"Hey, you're right." Dustin meeting my pale ale with a tink of his High Life bottle.

"I'm *right*."

"But that's what love is, my man.

"Disrespecting Jimbo?"

"Disrespecting *yourself*."

So there it was, is, and that's really all that we can ask. Loo*k at yourself*, I tell myself, and do, just for a second glancing down at the scene: my dinky dated bathroom, my lion pants on the floor, the bathtub dirty and stained, the shower curtain mildewy, pubes violently scattered around the base and back of the toilet, me sipping coffee that is almost cold as my cheeks go about their intermittent flapping.

Across town is somebody who loves me? This? Who at one point, right after we had first started dating, on one of those magical first-ish mornings, when the sun is always shining and her bed felt warm, left-on-the-counter-butter soft, had sealed all unspoken deals? She'd been floating about the apartment—floating it always seems in the nascent days, making me feel rather Lothario-like, endowed-ish, macho in a loveable Jack Lemmon way—doing errands and going about the opening and closing of closet doors and chopping in the kitchen and listening to the radio and drinking juice and humming, occupied with the things that people who get up on the business side of noon do. I was hungover, wine hungover, because such sophomoric relationship stages require wine, something poetic, romantic, classy, French, almost Proust-ish. Through half-open eyes, I remember her coming in and taking the near-empty glass of water from the nightstand. I was thirsty, cotton-mouthed, starting to roll over in the tangled web of soused sheets, not ready to get up, to speak, but thinking, "If she brings me a glass of water, I'll marry her."

I heard the faucet before the thought was done, X psychically-tuned to my liver, to my dehydration, to my undeserving need to not walk alone forever.

All the words on New Orleans are better than that? My worldview and poor man's poetry and, forgive me, *food reviews* should take precedence? Over a heartfelt hangover glass of water from someone with long, flowing Italian-ish hair that tumbles out of a winter hat while walking Michigan Ave with a cocoa at Christmas time? Who likes to go out to eat, to places of my picking? Who is employed in an office-type situation of reliable elevators and college degrees, and has some dough and a spot in Lincoln Park and will be seen in public with me, eating wood-fired pizza and laughing at my jokes, on a Friday night?

There's almost enough there, enough to say *fuck it*, to go toward domestication and quiet Saturday nights and quiet condo sex—satiny-sheeted, polite, after-shower clean. Retired, shoulders-shrugging, but in a good way, intimate. The same feeling arises from the new absence of Smoke, the echoing silence hitting and halting. I almost miss his barrel-chested bravado and knock on the door—a friend in all situations—from my little throne. Or it could be his progress, and the fact that the thought of movement, of *moving* and *change*, has always given my heart fits and flourishes, since back when Mom announced Buffalo was no longer the place for us, and my Bills fandom would need to take place halfway across the country. I've preferred a stationary stance, horizontal when I can, slouching when I can't. This is why I sit sometimes on the toilet until I can't feel my legs, circulation long gone, pins and needles awaiting me when I stand.

It's time to get that, something, going. Now or never, I tell myself, actually mutter it aloud, under my breath, with my pants down around my ankles and pasty black hair-flecked loafs of thighs jutting out before me—it's a terrible scene we play out in our private little moments—and the equally pasty top bulb of belly-buttoned fat covering over the vacuous dark hole beneath, leading to terrible places, through the hair and the smell that a shower never fully kills. It's why doors and locks were invented, and why roommates have to have something in the bank, in the savings account even, a 401(k) of kinship, to make it all work.

And here I sit, between roommates and editors, cities and life epochs.

This has been a nice interlude. I stand and hit the knob, crossing my fingers for a non-plugger-upper, looking forward to fixing the manuscript, and my life. Admitting said niceness implies it's over, and I'm already getting nostalgic for that time when you first come in and the seat is cold, and you have to flip back a few pages to remember where you were during yesterday's office hours, and you first hear the faucet, and the vent fills your earholes, and the world and society melt away, and the coffee is still hot and you sip deep. You sit deep. I have gone all-in today, as I did yesterday and will tomorrow, whole-hogging it and thinking about calling Smoke to tell him as much. This moment is as close to epiphany as possible, the biggest realization how much left there is to figure out. Go, do a thing, care. *Make a sports play.* Now though, rising, ignoring the tingle through the thighs and the numbness below each calf, first I need to bang around under the faucet to find the plunger.

18. TED'S HOT DOGS
2312 Sheridan Dr.
Tonawanda, NY 14150

People like to call it *Theodore's on the Lake*, in theory because that's the original name, but more so because it's funny to be fake-pretentious about the whole enterprise. Like the mispronunciation of Target, where people love to say 'Tar *jay*,' going up at the end, all fake Frenchy-like. Or people saying *internets* or *interwebs*, or something that isn't what they mean but is longer and nonsensical, *aww shucks* silly, full of pretend humility. These things become their own things, carried on the winds of social media or the vernacular or something from a rap video, it being on one day and the kids saying it the next and their parents after them in a pseudo-ironical way that they think implies a subtle hipness because they can laugh at themselves but, by saying whatever the thing is, actually shows they know what is going on.

What the kids are saying.

It's exhausting, trying to keep up. You'd need to make a list, remember to keep after said list, try to not get exhausted with the keeping of the list, the updates, ever expanding. Around us the irony flows, and ebbs. Proust would be so confused.

But they get more words if they don't *use an acronym. All the time with the acronyms these days!*

Fuck, Marcel, I told you, brevity is in these days. You and all those words...

But the magic, the rhythm, the flow of the...

Obvs, dog. Obvs.

On the irony runs, like the ketchup here at Ted's. You order a side of fries and make for the pit stop station with the napkins (forks, too, for some reason) and the big vat-like tubs of ketchup. Catsup, emphasis on saying *cat*, if you want to be modernly dickheaded about matters. There's a big pump, severe in its height, and you put your palm to the top, push toward hell, and fill one of those tiny paper dip sauce holders. Then you fill another. And another. You'll probably only use two, but you'll want at least five, to make sure, so you don't have to get up once you get your dogs in front of you on the big tray. The flimsy paper feels soft and smushy as they fill, and it is the ultimate eating anomaly, that a truly great food, to be enjoyed, needs a side of *something else*. But the fries aren't really that good here, a bit stringy, could use more salt. You have them anyway, and between bites of what you are truly after in life, they afford time to ponder, to reflect, to gain perspective on your hot dog. It is a great drawing out, to be appreciated. Like the longest philosophical aside before you get back to the action. If there is any action, plot.

But is there *plot* in life?

Here at least, what you are chasing, what they *do*—in the cocktail party sense of the word, where you have to have a single word or acronym label or aggressive verb to sum up your existence on Earth—is hot dogs. People like to refer to hot dogs as "encased meats." It's funny, high-brow, something you can easily fancy up and then overcharge for. Give them fun names, make sexual double entendres about how they are wieners. Put some kimchee on top. Or there's the other way to go, toward the nostalgia for a "dirty water dog," slumming being something else. *Ahh, the magic of New York streets. Like how it was back in the 70's.* As long as it's kind of gross and pre-cooked by an angry or indifferent Armenian and then you get to put your own listless toppings on, the neon yellow mustard on the sad soggy bread. It is a real capital-E Experience, anyone with the pleasure of having been to New York a couple of times and then put into the esteemed position, the getting into the spotlight of *Let me tell you about New York*, will tell you.

Because you've been?

I have! It's funny you should ask!

I've never been able to tell whether this hot dog bit is actually passive or active irony, but it is the same sort of people who look back on the yesteryear days and get sentimental over carjackings and crack—people who weren't there, or are full of shit, or were smoking crack. But such socioeconomic, anthropologic, gastronomic insights don't need to be noted in a cultural bit covering Tonawanda. They don't exist on Sheridan, not with Ted's, nor with the donut shop across the street, which is next to Caputi's, and next to another bar that resembles Caputi's, except the wings there are "Cajun"—very good, actually, now that I think on it. There's something missing with the bartendress situation, though, and thus I've only been four or five times in what has, so far, been a five-week residency.

People create intricacies and make things complicated, as people are generally the worst. That's the real thing I'm concluding, nodding to myself as it comes poetically, fisting and unfisting my non-eating hand around a napkin. This happens as I sit at a picnic table, tucked away just enough from the street, a stone's throw from Grandma's, under the red-print-on-yellow-background sign, fronted by a soda cup that has an encased meat on it—the poor bastard in a chef's hat and apron and bow tie, smiling, standing on what looks to be some very hot coals, gesticulating to the name Ted's with what appears to be great pride in the product. This would qualify as cannibalism, if the hot dog is in fact signifying another one of his kin, or, maybe it is self-eating, since he is in fact roasting at the very moment and looking quite content. How's that for irony?

Ha, I think to myself. Actually say it to myself as it dawns on me, and I wipe mustard from one thumb, lick it from the other, and pick up the pen to make a note of such.

It is early December and unseasonably warm, and I'm reveling in distance from Ike, Johnny, the lot of them, having even left my cell phone at Grandma's, appreciating being the weirdo to everyone inside the joint, the guy deep-throating foot-longs, taking notes, laughing to himself, occasionally talking to Proust, lighting up mid-meal and ashing in the half-black melting snow. Ted's might be my first love, and surely Freud would have something to say to that, something to the effect that it set me up, implied coming greatness, in terms of prose, and eating.

But I can't get enough of the weiner's here. They are sourced locally, the term still applicable even if it's from an industrial meatpacking plant with no windows. Over the big brick charcoal fire they cook each one to order, to your specifications, get them about half-black, charry, slit them with the pokers in three strips to allow pressure to escape, let the skin turn Rosacea red and wrinkly. They will toast the bun too, if you want, which you very much do.

You get them on the tray when they are still steamy, warmth and diverse color toppings seeming to offset Buffalo skies: near-fluorescent relish, glistening pickle, neon yellow horseradish mustard that tastes and looks like it has something to prove, all professionally splayed with confident teenage hands as you order. The hot sauce is what truly starts the engine though, with a zing, a rev, a *c'mon girl* yielding desired horsepower results on a cold January garage morning. There's something approaching foodie-ness about the savory mixing with the sweet herein, a secret housemade concoction some talking gut would laud on one of those food porn TV shows and subsequently inspire future fatness voyages. It's something I could fetishize, pontificate all Proust-ish about. Johnny swears by it, as did O.G. Johnny and I am now, not fully understanding, just continuing and going all-in with the crackle snap of the skin, the garlic running with the nostalgia, the ketchup adhering to the char, coal leaving its cremated ghosts to dance about my tongue.

Footlongs are the best play, though if you want to experiment with topping combo variations—cheese, onion, jalapeno; mustard, onion, hot sauce; *everything*—a case could be made to just get four or five regulars. Variety being the life spice, as they say. Grandma informs me they've even started serving burgers. Knowing what they do, how to warm up meat, how to make it saucy and team it with carbs, they must certainly be great. If I had more time—*more time, dammit!*—I'd give one a shot, a whirl.

That said, new orders in old towns are difficult. The aforementioned nostalgia, for what Ted's used to mean in childhood after a baseball game, before Dad got too drunk, the red sun of summer still up and Johnny and I on our way to sit on the big four-seater swing in Grandma's backyard, with the promise of Jim Kelly coming back in the fall. Also, there's a pissed-off defiance in the air as I grab my tray and head back toward the line. A double-header, why not? I'm getting another footlong, yes, who's judging me? These dickheads with their irony and acronyms? This one's for Grandma, anyways.

Yes, she's going to deep throat it, jerks. HaHa. With her clitoris!

There's something personal at Ted's. I feel it now more than ever, as if it never occured to me, a proper noun up there on the sign that hits close to home. A possessive apostrophe after my name. My place, *motherfuckers*. Go home with your snarking mockery and half-grinned derogatory condescension and clever facial hair and satirical hats. Theodore's it is not. I'll get three, four orders if I want, and chow them with all the authentic depravity in the world.

Food rancor moves me, pummels sensitivity. Here is my place in the world, and what am I doing with a pen and paper? How can one criticize objectively, subjectively, whichever is which—I can never remember, I'll have to fake it with that lesson to Dustin—who they really are? Why can't we just appreciate ourselves and the flaws, the fatness? This is an article that maybe shouldn't be written, nobody deserving of knowing. To think of dickheads from Iowa—and why is it that know-nothing Iowans are always ruining matters?—

or even my neighbors in Chicago, who think they know something about encased meats, them reading my lofty flights and wanting a try, to get a piece, to have another notch on the belt, why do they get to know, to see me fat-gutted, naked, my history laid bare?

Maybe none of these should be written. There is no explaining Mighty Taco, or the pepperoni at Bocce's, and the way that the cheesestuff melts over the meatstuff when you're hometown buzzed and it's 4AM in a booth at Jim's. Or over the coffee table at Helka's, with pants off, with Jim's *and* Mighty Taco. The book would be too long—to describe going home again, and bellying up with your brother, slurping suds and not enough air to cool the burning, scorch-crisp skin of Dad-favorite chicken wings while the bartender laughs and takes off his glasses and rubs his temple thinking about the Bills. Besides, nobody even reads books anymore, and as for critics, who is not one? As they say.

"But people still read me, right?" Proust asks, beside me, munching, stopping for a second, looking wide-eyed and pathetic in a hurt way I've never seen out of him, some ketchup dribbling down his gray chin whiskers.

"Oh yeah, dude. You're still a big deal."

"Oh." He's placated somewhat, but worried, too, dragging more fries through the ketchup, unsure of himself for a change, self-conscious, reposed, distant. As if he were for the very first time considering his own mortality. As if it had never occurred to him that at one point not only would he not be here, but his work would be ignored, his life and name forgotten. Everyone he'd ever known, dead. The first time I'd considered O.G. Johnny's forthcoming death, him being an old man, me being eight or whatever, old enough to understand that old men get old and then older and then too old and then they are dead, it had never previously crossed my impish mind. Not until after Super Bowl 26, when O.G., heartbroken, a bit loosened by an extra Super Sunday Vodka Squirt and a bit deflated by the late-night hour, let it go.

Grandma tried, said, "They're good, they still got Jimbo and Thurman. They'll be back!"

To which O.G. replied, "But when? Who knows? I might not be around much longer!"

They *were* back, and then they were back *again*, but by that point the reverse whammy was snowballing. It hit me then, the sand slipping through the fingers, or whatever, each subsequent Super Bowl further cementing it, getting us all one step closer to a surely disappointed death.

"Look, *everyone* still knows your name," I tell Proust, dragging my fries through the fallout on the paper partition in front of me, the leftover mustard and sauce and onions from my second footlong.

"Yeah?"

"OK, a lot of people."

"Oh." He tries a smile with the corner of his mouth, looking sadder for the effort.

"Look, I know who you are, motherfucker. Whaddya want?"

"Can you explain to me again why irony is such a thing?"

"Why'd you do it? What's it all for? That's what you wanna know, isn't it?"

"I know why I did it. I think. Do you?"

"Why I did it?"

"No. We're still talking about me. It's not all about you, Teddy."

"Oh. Sorry."

"But I did happen to read some of your New Orleans book."

"Sucked, right?"

"Well…there were some parts…"

"Sentences were too long?"

"Not that."

"It had no point, right? That's it? No plot, just rambling."

"Well..."

At this I grin, and he grins, shrugs his shoulders, and I'm picking up my third footlong of the day—the one I had ordered to take home to Grandma, this one covered with magma-ish running yellow cheese and hot sauce, this one killing the twenty I had been yielded by my benefactor, rendering a balance that needs to be finished off with a debit card. Spending it all and then some, I feel my stomach flare as I shake my head at the profound, divine comedy of it all.

"Hey, Proust, *Divine Comedy*, that's one of your books, right!?"

"No, Teddy. No."

And I'm thinking I'm glad there are hot dogs, and post-hot dog naps, and good solid friends like Proust, whom I've never read and probably never will, to make everything a bit more bearable.

19. BUFFALO (5-7)

I'm on the toilet when the thought occurs. And lo, the hero chapter, possibly? Matriculating with a rumble, and a splash?

It comes before the wiping, after business time, when I'm still pouring over the Buffalo News and sipping bad Grandma coffee and getting pissed as up and down the columns the pundits are punditing, clamoring for a cleaning, a cleaving, asking to fire or release or burn at the stake everyone in the whole God-forsaken, crumbling Bills house, with its bad foundation and questionable pipes. I'm having one of those sports fan moments of irrationality, of too-personal attachment, rubbing the top of my hair—thinning by the day now, probably due to the reading material at-hand. It is frustration epitomized, a sort of fist-shaking non-understanding. Anger at God, questioning his hands and motives, comes quick and easy for Bills fans. There is the deep desire to do a thing, something—some kind of *sports play*—but, uncomfortably, parasitically alongside this, is knowledge that there is nothing to do, that you're too far removed, despite your pasty balled fists, and the only possible action is futilely punching a wall, cursing Norwood again, and maybe asking Dustin what he thinks. Also heavy, heavy drinking. But there is something else to do—it hits me as the vent that O.G. Johnny installed runs, echoing around the outdated bathroom fixtures, and with the faucet on, hot water steaming, and with Grandma in the other room, growing perturbed at the strain I'm placing on her old lady bladder, it not quite used to house guests tying up the amenities with 45-minute purges—something so simple:

We find Jim Kelly's house, and we knock on the door.

The seed had been planted some time back. Johnny's been hinting at taking a ride, mentioning vaguely a guitar shop in the southtowns, and I had countered with something about an Italian joint I'd recently read about (with meatballs no less, cooked with garlic even), thinking I could corroborate such a journey, make it calorically worthwhile, more fodder for the story the editor has taken to responding about, though in abstract terms implying ignorance, disbelief, uncertainty. Something tells me he doesn't know I've left town, and it's not something, but his very specific mention that I might drop by the office to go over a few things, flesh out some new ideas, perhaps revisit the Pilsen taco scene, do the whole 'New' Maxwell Street Market number, wax poetic on who's got the best brunch burger, the spiciest kimchee, the most awesome roasted garlic dish. He wants to get some deadlines concreted for the future, some thinkpieces percolating, some ideas running through ideation, the type of "action" such men need for justification of their bookish life of letters. Something to suggest and then let echo and then adjust thick rim glasses to. Some ideas, some *Chicago* ideas, though I'm not in Chicago, and don't know if I will be anytime soon, or ever again.

I'm not sure why I'm here, nor why Johnny is still here, nor Ike, for that matter, though Ike is just drifting around the periphery of all laid plans, like an out-of-work boxer. Scooting in for a jab, testing the waters, scoping Helka's fridge for leftovers, and then heading back out toward undisclosed activities, his guard up, face and privacy protected.

I guess I don't know why anyone is still in town—that goes for Helka, too, and the regulars at Caputi's. It will be Christmas soon, and the Bills are causing communal, seasonal gastric distress that has nothing to do with Christmas, or even chicken wings, and everything to do with a year-end losing streak and a subsequent need to see Jim Kelly. Something about the juju, the vibes, the jism, whatever voodoo-leaning psychological *whammy* Helka would confuse it as, filtered through Proust and a sprinkling of old lady Teressa, the latter hating everything she stands for now, as wings are eaten with spite and empty comfort-seeking in the cooling shadow of that false early season promise. As the wind turns cold, and God remembers, and another long, barren, slushy-stepped January, February, and March careens toward us.

Johnny's friend and former bass player, Jon, has a work friend whose cousin's drug dealer's babysitter has a definite, verifiable, almost-positive address for Jim Kelly's Orchard Park homestead. Near the stadium, close to the magic, next door to reason enough to hop in the car and leave for a bit, skirt downtown bigness and breathe outside Helka's DNA-dented stuffy house. And so, just like that, up and out, away from Tonawanda, from Caputi's, on a distinctly Buffalo day where the gray is swirling and the streetside snow is blackening, rockifying, necessitating parking safe distances away from the curb to avoid the hammer-like crunk against soft fiberglass when passenger doors are opened. The heat is humming in the Malibu and our windows are cracked, 97 Rock waxing and downright buffing the nostalgia with bad Bad Company and some heart-rending Dire Straits. We're moving toward the river and then down, almost like a Springsteen song, the one about going down, or being on fire, or something we can't recall as "Sultans of Swing" hits and we think about our father.

"It was his longest kick on grass, you know that?" I say, evoking sadness when the need for chain-smoking in the car comes over me. Or vice versa.

"You're talking about Norwood. You're doing that fucking thing where you go into non-sequiturs about Norwood. The out-of-nowhere tirade about a Bills placekicker that last played 20 years ago. You're leading off a conversation with a random factoid about Norwood, Teddy. Fucking Norwood." Johnny hits the wheel with his palm, shaking his head, grimacing in a laughing kind of way. Or vice versa.

"I'm just saying, John. I don't think it was his fault."

"There's no fault, Ted. It's a make-or-miss moment. Poof. Done.

Gone." Johnny levels his hand out, sweeping it wide with the histrionic flourish of a preacher, indicating infinity.

"47 yards, man. That's all I'm saying. You can't blame him."

"Who's blaming?"

What you are supposed to feel at church, if raised in that kind of family, is community, possibly inspiration, and things like divinity, purpose, answers; some sense, amidst all the hullabaloo and ragtag cantankerous madness pulsing from above and around. Bills Sundays used to be like that. O.G. Johnny would hold court in his little office, tucked into his chair with head cocked and hands folded gently over his genitals, wearing Grandpa pants with the crease and a Bills sweatshirt without a hood. Having digested the sports page and three cups of joe, he'd get gently nervous, bemused with excitement, brow furrowed as Helka clamored around the room and set up TV dining trays for the holding of various foodstuffs: pepperoni slices, cheddar cheese wedges, something packaged, stuff with salt, tooth-picked bits of protein, Velveeta-gooped carbohydrates, and then later, around halftime, pizza and wings. He would get excited by the second quarter, when the *whammy*ing would take hold, and Bruce Smith would have worn his guy down to start the cavalcade of large black man acts performed in the opposing team's backfield. Grandpa would eventually venture a nibble, loosen up, go to the kitchen to reward himself with a Vodka Squirt. He'd shuffle back to the room looking pleased, sipping out of a straw with a bendable neck. He'd urge, quietly at first, and then building, a "Blitz!" He'd hope for a turnover, or declare a "big play" coming up, and it would be like a prediction for the Bills to do the thing, the requisite, obvious *sports play*.

Games would be watched after church, but that church was given little thought, even while you were there and doing that thing where you brush your thumb against your forehead and then chin and then something else, it seeming simply to exist as a time to collect, gather thoughts, get the Sunday yawns out, a pregame stretch, just show up to ensure that God knew as to which was the proper side. Looking back I see this moment as us in pregame mode, standing in the tunnel, rolling our heads, lightly bouncing in place, the scene before the big game in a sports movie, the one where Dad comes out and says the last inspirational thing so the viewer knows, later, when the director cuts to him right before the big play, just how proud he is, how vindicated, how that stoic look isn't gas.

But one week God caught a bus, or a train—the Empire Builder perhaps, screeching roughshod through Albany, away from all the little lakes, toward the Big Apple. Everything seemed to change overnight, or maybe that day, during the newfound time to kill before the big game, the Super Bowl played at night, and so there was time for the fateful trip to Family Tree.

And then everything changed again the week after. Me and O.G. had just gotten done watching the Pro Bowl. Johnny stayed home in protest, watching the Sabres with Dad. I took gentle solace from the first Super Bowl loss in Helka's roast beef and a side of wings, and the fact that half of the AFC team was made up of Bills stars, or so it seemed. And then Mom had come with the news. She didn't know how to say it, appeared to not know how to talk. From afar, from the perspective of one watching a sad movie, you could see Little Teddy there in the back seat, with his feet pointing awkwardly inward still, though he was growing up and it was getting less pronounced. Putting some Buffalo winter weight on, becoming almost real.

Though I remember the Duff's of the day, the way the sauce glistened and the sucking sound my little mouth had to make instinctively after tangy bites, thinking air would help ease the tongue devastation, I can't recall exactly how Mom told us that Dad had ended it. There were Johnny tears, later, and air sucks of a different kind, but Teddy was quiet, just noting a shadow entering the car as it turned left on Sheridan, sweeping across the backseat and then out the other side, then there existing a new kind of diagnosis, a sudden resignation, something like Norwood, with bits of fist-making, waves of confusion, a quiet moaning hush, a big drop of cement hardening in the middle of all our backs.

"Fucking team is gonna be the death of me," I say, back in the moment, and it seems like I never really left, will never stop the tires from spinning in this exact Christmastime rut.

"You're not suicidal, right, Teddy?"

"Not until I see a Super Bowl win."

"You've got that backwards. It's a Super Bowl loss, then you wanna die."

"Nope. Dad had it backwards."

Johnny points the car and steers, each of us quieting.

"Ike still blames you, I think." I drop it quick and sudden, jutting my jaw out and scratching at the stubble. As much a warning as an indictment, but the indictment isn't on John at all, or even really on Ike for being an asshole. It's on all of us, for being messed up in the missed-kick business, the sunken ship for which we refused lifeboats. It's an indictment for us being back here, now.

Johnny says nothing, just stares ahead, drumming his fingers now as Charlie Watts hits with the *bah-dah* opening groove of "Honky Tonk," the Stones always coming on 97 Rock when you need them, unless it's the Allmans or ZZ, or else it's something bad that makes you laugh and get condescending, like the assholes at Ted's I could hear in my head as I went up for further footlong insertion.

"Speaking of the longest," Johnny says, tapping the brakes, changing the subject, "I think the other week was your longest leap on grass."

"Yeah, that was something." I wipe a tear from the corner of my eye, pat my tit pocket and realize I'm out, the trip to the Promised Land longer than I remembered, the need for smokes, the fidgeting, greater.

"You got some hops."

"I feed off the hometown crowd energy."

"And how you didn't drop the burritos…"

"I just don't want to let the fans down."

At this we're laughing, covering up despair with volume, chesty exhales and exposed teeth, before devolving to reposed grimace-smiles, our death mask.

"Do you know what we're gonna say when we get there?"

"I'm going to explain the situation, and he's going to grant us luck and absolution."

"Like the Pope?"

"Yes. But, ya know, better. Like Jimbo."

Ahead there's hope of shiny guitars with big price tags, and the chance I can hear Johnny play one for a minute, close my eyes, and forget all the bumping Boston and our hateful diety. There's the promise of meatballs afterward, too. Diversion. As we get off the freeway into Orchard Park, the Malibu feeling like it knows the way to go, Johnny is lighting two cigarettes in his mouth and handing me one. There is that, and there is Jim Kelly's house, most definitely just around the corner.

20. CHICAGO (5-1)

It's never easy getting up, out to the suburbs, especially one as far north as where Mom lives. Not without a car. And as the cabbie—so out of place so far outside of the city—negotiates long boring boulevards from the train station amid the homogenization that equates to middle class success and, also, finally, resignation, I gaze out the window, calm, placated, numb. This could be my plot, life amongst these biggish houses on large lots, and the strip malls with their pizza places and workout places and places to get your eggs, all fronted by parking lots. Nobody walks. Anyone who does would seem to be leaving the scene of a broken-down car. Except everyone out here has a new, Japanese car, so this never happens. There are no bars, except at weird crossroads where places like Route 41 intersect major streets like Grand Avenue, and they are outside of town, in weird nether regions that sometimes approach some municipal monstrosity deemed "Unincorporated." They have neon lights, but almost no windows, and every time you pass you know that inside are one million forgotten high school names and faces—girls that put on weight, guys that grew goatees, everyone with more flab, less hope. The ghosts of expectation slow-dance around the wood-paneled room to Top 40 mainstream hip-hop or whatever that is, former winners reliving glory days of the field, the backseat, over bad beers and shots of Jager. Droopy meathead eyes from the arms-crossed bartender gazing over their shoulders, reliving on his own. Sports replays are always cycling, blinking on multiple budget-but-bright TVs. Magnavox or the Target brand. There's video poker, maybe a pool table below a leftover plastic display from the bar-hosted March Madness bracket—somebody named Gousha really nailed it with his Kentucky pick. There's the Bears schedule in proud display, ornamentation touting happy hour specials, fish fry specials, everything presented in a bad font and gaudy colors.

There is nothing to drink but Old Style, and not even Old Style in ironic form.

It is society between stratas, periods—a group of which I could probably consider myself part, being youngish and semi-employed, not living exactly *in town* but fresh enough to be recognizable—and they can't help but feel uncomfortable here. Men, women, border-line-adults, all without a country, and one can't help but yearn to get back to the city, where most everyone is young and there's something about dreams that are still possible, if only because most everyone is young and there are ten bars within walking distance and a skyline that plops itself into some days, sometimes.

I still get carded in the 'burbs, being of that indeterminate age that must harken closer to 18-or-under than 50-plus. Everyone is one or the other, except in those watering holes just outside of town, where hordes emerge from parents' basements after the sun goes down to belly up in Springsteen-ish fashion. And the bartenders, the cashiers, the gas station attendants, they don't seem to ever real-ize that before them is a *man*. A *full-grown* man, a full-grown man of letters. A man nearly able to comfortably afford half-an-apartment in a not shabby part of a major American city. A man *published*, oc-casionally. A man old enough to have friends that have kids. To know some people that have bought houses. A man who could buy a car. Or who could, possibly, show up to a dealership and be taken semi-seriously, not suspiciously, and even get a test drive out of the whole ordeal. A man nearly old enough to grow a beard, or at least some kind of dirty goatee.

So later, after the cab and pocketing some 20s from Mom, I'm pulling out my ID at the Piggly Wiggly, ringing up two sixers of a new Goose Island IPA and keeping my head down as I ask the check-out girl, with not a single *chalant*, for a pack of Camels. She probably goes to my alma mater, or just got done, and is enter-ing the moving-to-the-basement phase, or else the moving-to-the-city-with-her-girlfriends-and-getting-a-job-waitressing phase. Neither as exciting or depressing as they once seemed, each looking now like a simple shoulder-shrug approach to late-teen living, the placeholder, the bookmark in a rather bland book with too long sentences and no real point. I could impart this wisdom, let her in on the forthcoming disappointment, the inevitable cavalcade of Friday-to-Monday, and the walk back down the hill. I could hip her—as they say, if they still say—to all the friends she will lose, how few she'll gain. How familiar the bars will become, so fast, suddenly so unsexy.

Or I could mention our probably-shared high school. Just like that, ask her how goes ol' Rooney, or some such-named inspirer of yesteryear. Ask her about the latest sexual misconduct allegations facing some administrator, someone with a name like Raker, who you think would have been implicated pre-transgression, based solely on such a foretelling moniker. Ask her if my picture still hangs on the wall—always in dreams somebody's putting my picture up on the wall, though I'm not quite dead. I could ask her what time she gets off.

So what time you get off?

(Blushes.)

I could buy us some beer.

(Face blood vessels dilating, or whatever it is they do.)

Maybe get us a hotel room.

(Swoonful eye-batting, possible moist clitoris.)

Her: *Umm, you have a car?*

Me: *It just so happens I got my mom's...*

We start a fling. Everything kicks off simply enough, with a bottle of Vodka and a third floor room at the Ramada. I duck down to the vending machine to wrangle up some mixers, then some ice. She sheepishly bites her lip and sits on the edge of the bed as I come back through the door I've left open, laid against the flippy

138

metal inside door lock, the move of a seasoned hotel-stayer. She's never been in one aside from with her parents and that one time she went to D.C. for a high school choir trip, which was when she first got drunk, which she didn't like but wants to try again. I'm gentle, patient, and she groans a lot once she loosens up, the vodka doing its work. She listens to my thoughts on Bob Dylan with great interest and Lolita eyes before the moaning foreplay. I talk earnestly, with arms outstretched in *can't you see* gesticulation. Four days later we're still there, my phone turned off and resting on the floor. The Weather Channel is on, the blinds are drawn. There are bottles in various states of abuse, in multiple sizes, mostly cheap-ish and plastic—Smirnoff, Cuervo, etc.—whatever I can score at the gas station next door that has a liquor aisle and non-judging attendant. For a high school girl she is into some dirty stuff, some of which makes it hard to look her in the eye the next day, but she's green and excitable, and is eighteen years old, with an eighteen-year-old body.

She's always stretching her arms out wide and smiling at me, and we talk about how we'll go to her parents, explain the situation, and our lust, how she's too young for me but how immature I actually am, so it evens out. We know they won't approve, but we'll sit in their parental kitchen, surrounded by her framed senior pictures—taken three months ago—and we'll hold hands, and eventually I'll win over her dad with my deep-seeming devotion and our mutual enjoyment of basketball.

We'll have kids, and she'll start singing again when the tykes go off to school, and we'll have a little library in the front room of our Lincoln Park brownstone where I'll sit and read Keats or Goethe and tug on my beard while she knits and Vivaldi—no, fuck that, *Blonde on Blonde* plays soft from the next room.

But too much time is spent not wanting to be seen, hood up, eyes shifty, me the post office wall picture of Ted Kaczynski, and by the time I even think of the opening line, realize how little chance there'd ever be for Lindsey or anyone else in Chicago to find out, I'm already back in Mom's sure-starting and ever-running Honda, hoping to avoid sedan-seeing anyone cruising in 5MPH endless parking lot mode, lest they see me lighting up, those former tennis coaches and fellow semi-smart kids catching me desperately trying to get all the smoke plume out the window of the Accord, lest I draw Mom's chagrin. It would take all of them just one of these glances to know precisely the foul-smelling, fire-breathing miscreant I'd become. The kind I had, always would, come back to be, bumping at a reasonable volume the Chicago classic rock station — always 'Stairway' or 'Rain Song', always so sad, sadder here, home, though a home once-removed — as I'm headed back down slightly familiar nondescript cookie cutter subdivision streets, just hoping for some more womb time.

If I could just crawl back in there for a bit…

The problem, that which has rendered me up a handful of zip codes outside the city on a crisp fall Friday night when I should be preparing for a big Sunday game with a big Friday night of beer and game film and corner bar boasting with Dustin, is that I'm about to have nowhere to live. There are options, of course, prime among them cohabitation and its subsequent appeal of turning a sometime sex partner into a full-time roommate, one with whom you almost never have sex, busy instead arguing about taking out the trash or doing the dishes or not having enough sex, and who *the fuck* ate the last piece of pizza, or how much time is too much time spent drinking with Dustin on the couch. At least this is how I see it, casting my life and my habits in the mirror, as I force myself to do every now and then.

"Guess I haven't done much with my life, Ma," I say, stoic, cracking my second Goose, picturing myself, in my knit cap, Nicholson or some such heartbreaking winner of the loser role in 70s flicks. "I might ask Dustin to live with me, but he's, like, engaged, I guess?"

The summer Saturdays we might have, game day and her jitters far enough away, and the sunny Sundays, too, when it's hot and there's nothing to do but avoid that sun as best as we can. I like to sleep in, and the hangovers will be NFL-concussive, but I like to make Dustin happy even more, so I'll set my alarm, brush it off before it creates too much racket and wakes him, my new roommate. I'll go to the kitchen and get the French Press going, scoop in five reckless spoonfuls. I can see myself humming as I heat up some oil, chop onions, jalapenos, mash garlic with the side of the knife like it's the Food Network. Warm tortillas and wrap them in a little towel like it's Oaxaca. Pour the salsa in a bowl and put it on the island, put some chips right by like it's Instagram. He'll eventually wake to the smell of bacon, and that's when I'll start the French Press, pour him a cup when I get done beating the egg yolk, which I have tinted with smoked paprika. We'll guffaw over the previous night's misadventures, wide-eyed. Bemoan the hangover, *har har* over slurred words and forgotten lines.

I said that aloud!?

You said it really loud.

I'll learn to make hollandaise—what is hollandaise? In any event, we'll leave the dishes piled in the sink afterward, let the bacon grease solidify in the pan on the stove, and I'll make us second rounds of coffee and then we'll retire, like it's a Victorian novel, to the living room, where I'll lay on the floor with my palms folded over my gut and a bedroom pillow under my bean. He'll get deep in the couch grooves, and we'll watch HGTV or ESPN before we doze off and pass the afternoon in varying degrees of consciousness.

This is what Mom and I are discussing, over beers. Well, over beer and wine, actually. She's sipping a Pinot, though I'm pretty sure she's not pronouncing it right.

"Nothing ever goes my way." I plop back down next to the fire, picturing Dustin all those miles away, looking around for me and my takes at what's become our Friday spot.

"Isn't it about time for a condo or something?"

I can't take the question seriously, still having not fully deciphered the difference between my current half-empty residence, and said C-word. It seems about that chapter, though, the chapter in life for knowing such things, the time arrived for a paragraph cluster of *figuring stuff out*. An upbeat movie montage of bullet-pointed accomplishments, lists with items crossed off in bold, bleeding permanent marker. A time one day we'll look back on from a moment of deserved repose, offer some kind of "salad" metaphor for the distant period. The "we'll" refers to a big family—happy, hearty, my son the star of his high school basketball team, my daughter with an eating disorder but smart and passionate about French studies, or international affairs, or journalism, or something equally useless to all but early 20-somethings. We'll stand around just such a fire as this, and they'll gently rib me—the grand patriarch!—about why I haven't written more novels before we pause for photographer-shot Christmas card pictures.

We teeter-totter over reality, Mom easing back on the couch as I smoke cigs and blow plumes into the fireplace. She avoids bringing up the book with all of its lofty white-privileged young man thoughts on death and America and mayonnaise and hot sauce. This is what it was supposed to be, anyway, though by the end the sentences were running away from themselves like they were guilty of something, something the *The* or pronoun or whatever word was capitalized at the beginning of the sentence knew, and the rest of the words needed to put more distance between, to get away from. Our discussion avoids the chance that this will be my new home for a bit, if there's no publishing said novel, if the one with the glasses, the editor, on a golf course, chomping his cigar, standing leg-over-leg and leaning against his driver like jerks that play golf are always doing, that ultimate arbiter of happiness, validation, success—life's great impostors—deems it to be so. If he refuses the story and leaves me homeless, it could be like ordering a salad as an entrée, after your salad as a salad.

"How's your ulcer, honey?"

"Not bad."

"Are you eating soft foods?"

"No, no. Soft *shits*. I think the doctor said soft shits was the goal."

"Oh yeah? And?"

"Almost water-like."

"And I hear the Bills are winning, honey. Right?" I'm not sure how this image leads to thoughts of the Bills.

"The Bills are winning. Yes. Yeah. But, well, it's misleading."

They have been, the credit likely, obviously, belonging to Dustin and I's consummation, our new friend juju, the kind that leads to hugs after wins, the kind that lead to fat guy roommate fantasies. It is a string of success that last week saw Jackson stiff-arm a safety into sideline oblivion, and the week before Fitz didn't even throw an interception. It's been three weeks since they beat the Patriots and Freddie brought his kids onto the field in the postgame. Dustin and I, hands on our heads, looked at the TV and the falling confetti, and, "Ahhh, Freddie!" we both shouted in unison, tearing up a bit, needing to look away, smiling out of the corner of our mouths, a profound human element to our gladiatorial macho pursuits. This prefaced Dustin running from one end of the bar to the other, arms over his head signaling a touchdown, like it was the Super Bowl, or like it was one of those ubiquitous black-and-white pictures near the end of every book about World War 2. There have been minimal sights of Dustin pacing with nerves, back and forth, but many high-fives and smiling cigarettes smoked in Sunday sunshine with buddy-bought beers sweating expectantly back on the bar.

Days of triumph. All-afternoon bouts of poetic drinking on Milwaukee Ave. leading to late evenings and forgotten calls. Pats, so many pats, on the back, and us going to the bar for one another, cool-down beers where we let our pit sweat congeal, fan our shirts against our swampy, no-longer-nervous tits. I feel throaty and chesty as a London character, the wins and the vibes peering through to lengthen the shortening fall days.

But there is always another shoe to drop. I have no idea as to the province of this proverb but I'm sure it's something to do with Bills fandom and an always impending steel-toed boot to the dome, dropped from a great height. Actually, more like *thrown*, by a God who has forgotten us, and then remembers and says, "Oh my, wait a second, what have we here?" He reads the sports page in his robe on a Monday, over steaming Sanka or something like that enjoyed by real, real old people, adjusting his reading glasses, scanning the standings. "Oh, *har har har*, with Fitz!? Looks like my plan got away from me there for a second while I was over in all that Middle East and mass shooting biz. Ok now, where were we?" He goes through the closet, pushing back crisp hanging dress shirts with one hand and rifling through new boxes of rust-hued work Timberland's with the other. Looking for the heavy ones.

"Well, honey..." Mom says.

I hear this distantly as I gaze at the flames dancing about in the fireplace, Mom litanizing or theorizing or explaining away how life doesn't go according to plan. Something about lemonade, and I think about citrus and the high school girl and how screwdrivers would be a nice opening round in the hotel.

"You know what, sweetie..." she goes on, but I'm mostly lost in this poetry moment: hand on chin, smoke mystic and pronounced and framing my face against the fire's bright backdrop in the dark living room. The tortured stance one might capture in statue form someday, when society deems it time to go back to statue-making. This one for the front of my high school, next to the one of the kid who died in Iraq from friendly fire and behind the one of the steroid-user who played Triple-A ball and got decapitated in a drunken boating accident. The one for the underclassmen stoners, and for the moms who drop their freshmen off and glimpse it everyday before going home to their vibrators and Oprah, thinking, "Why was he so sad?"

"Well you know you can move in here, honey, if the little book or that story doesn't work out."

With this, I know what I have to do. I'll go home, to the other home, pack it in, or up, whatever they say in motivational greeting cards urging movement. I'll watch some late-night highlights, jot some notes, and call Grandma. Get a line on a flight to Buffalo, an advance on some airfare, a welcome mat pre-laid for me and my troublesome stomach. Soft shits are to be further sought. Even Mom seems to be right there with my line of thinking.

"They're gonna pay you for this Buffalo, what is it, a *food assignment*, right, honey?" Mom asks, hopeful.

"Ma. It's not about the money."

"Ok, honey. Do what you wanna, but don't stay up too late tonight. I'm going to bed."

"I'll do what I wanna and I'll stay up too late," I say, staying up late always my sort of general protest.

"Ok, Teddy."

"And you know what, *and* I'll get a pizza."

"Alright, sweetie. Sweet dreams."

Every *sweetie* dropped seems like a condemnation on my character, my autonomy, my manhood. "You forgetting something, Ma?" I ask, regardless.

"What's that sweetie?"

"You're gonna pay for this one, right?"

"You spent all the money from before, sweet T?"

I flash back on forking over the money for the six-packs and their security, for the smokes and their warmth, for the chance to interact and transact and forcefully project demented fantasies out

145

onto the unsuspecting world, onto the poor thing just doing her job, smiling, innocent, thinking me harmless and shy and maybe even borderline mature, semi-adultish.

"Yeah, Ma. And I'm gonna spend all of this, too."

21. ANDERSON'S FROZEN CUSTARD
2235 Sheridan Dr.
Kenmore, NY 14223

We used to come here summer nights after baseball games, the sweat still on my brow and, sometimes, on my lips, and the salt might mix a bit with the cream and sugar in a fleshly Epicurean taste fete. I would be in little kid cleats and funny pointless stirrups, with big league dreams either still firmly intact or solidly swept away, depending on the game's outcome. The sun going down, highlighting itself, pure possibility in the darkening warmness—more baseball, fireflies, or, *dear God*, hide and motherfucking seek!

These evenings would start before Dad went home and started to sip, and to watch the Yankees, and to clench and unclench his fists. This was all before Dad used Super Bowl 25 as an excuse to get out, and long before Dad was replaced by a stepdad who had business in places like Shanghai, Singapore, St. Louis, and was seemingly always in one of them whenever I went home for my drink-and-smoke-and-chat-and-pizza trips to Mom's plush confines, her cozy new life, almost womb-like, perfect for such life analysis, the pastoral backdrop a man needs to figure out where it all went wrong, and to get drunk whilst doing so.

Mom always liked the cinnamon at Anderson's, it being her flavor spirit, a reflection of the personality within. A sophisticated playfulness, a subtle spice, some might say, though it makes no sense to describe one's own mother's personality, not unlike describing the taste of water, and so I can't see it. When it was the flavor of the day, which it still seems to be an inordinate amount, she would be elevated in weird Mom ways that infrequently serve as reminders that they are people, too, moms. Not just drivers and payers for ice cream and pizza, but entities with tastes, favorite movies, preferred sexual positions, all those etceteras that make your head hurt if you think on them.

Little Teddy used to get the lemon ice. I heard once that it was an Italian thing, and fell in love because I wanted very much to be Italian, holding out hope that I'd one day learn how to cut pepperoni in those bowl shapes like the unseen Sicilian in back of Bocce's. How I wanted to be of the pizzeria culture, where you can talk with your hands and let your hair get greasy and everything was warm ovens and cool dream smoke breaks. This despite the fact that I am Polish, and was just learning that my cultural identity could be used against me in derision. I wanted to be black, too, and catch passes out of the backfield like Thurman, juke and get to the sideline, blow games open. Italian and black, pepperoni and athleticism, some kind of indefinable mash of cultures, hopes, and dreams.

Helka likes whatever she can get her hands on. Whatever whomever is borrowing her car will bring back home, back across Sheridan, in pint form for the freezer. Or sometimes, if she's lucky and it's a Friday night of generosity and overdue family time, said someone will drive her to Anderson's herself after a fish fry. Johnny does it, and I do it, too, occasionally. The two of us will get stuffed somewhere on beer battered cod and bread and butter, and I'll have a few, and we'll both pretend I'm OK to drive. Once to the parking lot I'll go to the stand, bring two cones back to the car, surprise her with the flavor and keep the change after she's rendered a twenty from a white envelope in her purse. We'll sit there like that, slurping, chowing, 97 Rock turned low, talking about Grandpa and Ike and the weather and the time the Bills almost won.

O.G. Johnny was similar. He seemed to be happy just to have something to do with his hands, to have something to put on his tongue, as long as it could all take place within the gentle swaying of the backyard swing. He'd cock his head to the side, turn the cone, analyze drippage, furrow his brow, not one to let his ice cream fall out in his lap. It would glisten in his gray mustache, and he would accentuate this for comedic effect. In between bites he might launch into a yarn, one with a punchline, something about the war, or the Harlem Globetrotters. A yarn that little Teddy, and maybe little Johnny, would lap up like the cream and sugar and frozenness melting before them in the July Buffalo sun.

Johnny's gut led him naturally to something called an "Arctic Swirl," a rip-off of something you can get at a big box ice cream emporium, one that anybody raised within walking distance of Anderson's had been weaned to hate and scoff at. It's a swirl-like homage to the Arctic, yes, if the Arctic is all Oreos and semi-soft frozen custard topped with piping hot fudge and pillowy whip cream that you dig and swirl with a plastic spoon and then get fat on. Johnny owes much to the Arctic, and to these treats in their plastic cups with the Anderson's cursive logo and pictures of cones floating about happily therein, seeming so innocuous. Those calories are the real reason I still won't wrestle him, why I head for the hills if he lowers the shoulder in "Bruce Smith Mode."

Ike doesn't really go for ice cream, his brow furrowed in consternation, him wondering, asking us, "Why would I want to do that?" He'll tolerate a stop after a dinner, but will always wait out the tonguing next door at Caputi's, half-scowling and sipping something from a rocks glass in a dark corner. And so he doesn't really mind Anderson's after all.

Teddy, as in full grown half-beard Teddy, back in Buffalo on break from his big city life, notebook in hand, thinks it's great and all, fine, nostalgia has its place. I can tolerate, pat on the head, go along with the custardy flow in a manner of slight, smirking condescension. Though I've outgrown childish pursuits, don't ever check my phone for a voicemail from the majors, 'member-when-ing has its time. Proust can't be wrong and ridiculous about everything.

"Now see, right there," Proust interjects, "you were just talking about little league, and your old man, and always with the Bills! What is so wrong, dare I say, about nostalgia!? You, who loves Kerouac, of all hacks! Ha!"

"This is my book," I remind him. "My story, motherfucker."

"It ain't but navel-gazing wankery, a semi-studied half-martyr who's playing at the great sufferer, and you know it."

I've never seen him like this. Bent out of shape, contorting, scowling, leveling one of those weird pens with the feather on top in my general direction. Accusatory. And after all we've been through. After he told me, "Never give up, no matter what." I was drunk and teary, picturing myself heroic, poetically misunderstood, sitting on Grandma's stoop and Ike had drank the last beer. All seemed lost.

"I don't know why you're being such a bitch about this, Marcel."

"Because you're a lousy fucking writer."

"Because I don't want to go on and on and on? Sometimes I just get so tired of the revelry, revelry, revelry. That's all."

"You'll never be published."

"You're the one that told me to never give up."

He pauses, licks his cookies 'n cream, gazing out and over my head. When he speaks, his voice is distant and dreamy. "I never said you should give up."

But the post-game ice cream cone is nonsense. The looking back and staring, mouth agape, can get you caught up, stuck in a rut. And really, why should someone stand in one of those 15 lines outside Anderson's for what you could get at Dairy Queen? Why should you fill an already-full gut with softened milkstuffs of empty calories that only render more wanting instead of satisfaction? Cocaine works the same way.

Especially when what Anderson's does right, really, is roast beef. Tender slices slathered atop buns decked out in salt bits. The meat is something—there's probably garlic in it, maybe even of the roasted variety. The horseradish, too, an ephemeral sandwich topper you can actually taste in your nose, in your sinuses, as much as your mouth. Sometimes you get too big a hit, an overly excited bite, and then you get mad at yourself, feel it creeping, and then singeing. And if you're standing up, maybe at one of those circular tables, towering over all the little leaguers with their post-game tonguing, you have to ball your fist around a napkin, and, if it's really bad, stomp your boots and twirl around in place, in anger. Why didn't you just get ice cream? So soothing. Why do they put so much of this stuff on? Bastards. Those little meat slinging geniuses of the same staffing agency utilized by Jim's, with greasy skin and stick-like forearms and old-fashioned paper hats. Poisoning, executing with horseradish. But—*ahhhh*—mouth open, tongue out, slurping at O2 for cooling effect, shaking your head at those *sonsofbitches* back behind the counter, it's thrilling, exhilarating, and the subsequent soothing comes, helped along by each swig of water, making way for another chance, another bite, another push to feel the blood flow, to feel a part of this battle, it making strength, character, something.

Little Teddy's palate used to have a hard time here. His sensitive stomach, too. Sure, he liked the salt, the seeds atop the hard bun. He'd lick the sodium diamonds off, open up the sandwich and pry apart some of the meat, pop it in his gullet, make enough of a dent to adequately rationalize to Mom that dinner was done and it was "ice cream time." Eventually, though, somewhere between all the tumult and the snow and the losses, he got hardened. The whiskey and the Camels and the Frank's and the more Frank's and then sometimes the Frank's Extra Hot, and now here I am. Stopping late night, sitting on the hood of the Malibu with one knee up, supporting my head on crossed arms, gazing poetically toward the old ice cream joint, like something out of American Graffiti. It's cold, and there are a few other people here, though the sense of community seems to have waned over the distance of memory. Still, I prop myself on the front of Grandma's car and smoke and await my beef.

Sometimes, when back home, I go to Arby's. There is little guilt, because it's more of an aesthetic indulgence, how I love to gaze forlornly at a Big Montana's cross section, such is the sight of folded meat a thing to behold. Roast beef layered like t-shirts in a drawer, a bit haphazard, but all that soft, welcoming cotton; and then layered back the other way, atop other roast beef, everything contained inside the perimeter of the bun, only some folds spilling outside the lines, hinting at what could be coming if you just press down a little, enough to make some of the cow juices ooze toward the outside, toward the mouth, a symbiotic mixture with the horse-radish, the two joining up for dangerous, popping gang work.

Ice cream is for children in baseball stirrups, and meek grand-mothers with Malibus who can't drive after dark. Roast beef is the grandest of all desserts, and Anderson's the king of the after-meal.

22. BUFFALO (7-8)

Just minutes prior, cruising back across Sheridan, quick-puffing a Camel on the short ride, I was contemplating the game, thinking about our chances of going 8-8. Talking myself into the excitement therein, at the notion of success. From far enough away, breaking even is somehow like coming out ahead. Not so bad, like the best possible adult life. So you need a roommate? At least you don't live at home, in your mom's basement, cruising suburban streets like a viper after hours, 'member-when-ing with whomever happens to be in town, nobody you even really like, friends out of convenience. Failing to launch, you put money away that you claim is for rent but will wind up going towards booze or, if you're lucky, future therapy sessions. So you smoke, and you wrote a shitty book, your only legacy for when the diagnosis comes from on high, it doing the Earth and her strained resources a favor. It's not heroin track marks, at any rate, or suicide, and the unruly burden on survivors left to get uncomfortable when somebody asks what happened, with the awkward head scratches and throat clears and delay and search for non-existent tragedy-explaining platitudes.

8-8. .500. Mediocrity. It's the circling back, the going all the way around the world the wrong way in order to arrive next door. Except with no lessons learned and neither a win nor a loss. Simply being. Existing. Like the masses, neither good nor bad. Like a photo of one of those NYC street moments of teeming mobs crossing an avenue, mulling, mewling between meals and sleeps. A job and a house and a lawn relatively responsibly mowed, and beer and a couch and baseball on the TV on a Tuesday. It's Sisyphus, or some Greek or Latin guy, lurking below the surface, if you look, though not the one that fucked his mother.

"He doesn't even live in Orchard Park!" Ike shouts, that's the first thing I hear when I come through Helka's front door. It brings me back, out of my daydreamy Bills pregame revelry into confusion, misunderstanding, reality. He's hovering in Johnny's face in the other room, bent at nearly 90 degrees, a weird crimson hue in the cheeks that generally implies daytime drinking or extreme constipation.

Of course Jimbo lives in Orchard Park, I think, where else would he live? Don't be ridiculous. After all, what were me and Johnny doing on that whole cruise, driving around, skipping out on Grandma and responsibilities, aimlessly pointing an old American auto nose and talking deep the way you do in a car, without eye contact, just sideways glances? Were we perusing the Southtowns just for some old fashioned meatballs we saw a guy on TV try? Was it strictly for the jubilant, mischievous feel of getting away with smoking in the Malibu, as if we were 17 again and proving to Mom that we were bad, that we were outlaws, by doing the exact same thing that she did?

Coming through the door I wonder if I smell like smoke, the ubiquitous plastic baggy from Anderson's dangling from my arm, bringing home custard, or ice cream, I don't really know the difference, another of those things I waited too long to ask about and now, being something of an adult, cannot. Anyway it's just a diversion, something to tide the rest of them over while I take my roast beef, covertly held under my shirt, and head back to Johnny's room to cravenly burn my sinuses with zinging horseradish while the tongue and acid work the salty bread bits into delicious spongy mush. It's my bit of covert ops, something like what I imagine O.G. Johnny was up to between photos back in the day in the tropics.

But there's tension here, a pulsing energy, emanating vibes, cartoon character stink lines. Grandma is in the O.G. seat, staring stoically out the window, fingers wrapped like old forgotten house ivy around a cooling coffee cup. She sees me and my bag and feigns a smile, but it's the victim smile, the Jodie Foster smile, the coroner's office smile, the hospital waiting room resignation of the family member tasked with being the strong one, the one refusing tissues and looking the doctor in the eye, taking it straight.

"Oh, Teddy," she says, "have some pizza, there's leftover Boc-ce's in the fridge."

"I gotta save that," I say. "For postgame."

"OK. Johnny's already ordered a pregame pizza."

"*And* I got you fat fucks ice cream!" I shout into the next room, applying, I hope, some throaty levity.

There's no response, only a kind of static, and I feel a drip of per-spiration roll down my right ribcage. Grandma continues to stare out the window, looking small, seeming to wish herself smaller, coiling, but I'll need her, her grandmother's strength, her octoge-narian sinew, should the swirling in the next room prove to be of the named-storm varietal.

Seemingly there is disagreement over the 'burb where Jim Kelly resides. Surely Jon's pot dealer's uncle couldn't be so wrong—or was it the uncle's pot dealer? But here it is, too late, suddenly game-day, with everything tilting and unpredictable like Thanksgiving dinner on the high seas and the horizon's darkening. Really, ac-tually, this is the funnel cloud, the absurd squelching noise from the Weather Channel indicating threatening barometric pressure, the stuff of school-closing blizzards. It isn't about where Jim Kelly parks his snowblower, it is about the horizon taking a turn for the worse, in every direction, as far as we can see.

Through the kitchen doorway I make out Johnny's knees, in his chair, pointing at Ike in a skewed, off-balance way, their stances those of boxers, even with Johnny seated, both of them angling, measuring. I will have to get in the middle. I will have to feign an ulcer attack. This, clearly, obviously, is the only way, the only appli-cable *sports play*: crumpling to my knees, clutching my chest, or, no, my gut. They will have to have hearts, at least one, collectively, be-tween them, and look on me with something approaching human-ity, pity. They will be so concerned as to my intestinal well-being that they'll forget the pent-up aggression, the blame, the frustration over death and Super Bowl failure and directions to a former great's current residence. Forget it all, to tend to little big-gut Teddy and his fragile, woeful health.

It's an attack. The ulcer. I'm the littlest, the youngest, our last chance at respectable heritage-making for the Rawski clan. There's a fluttering. I'm dying...

No, Teddy, you're just fat.

What's happening instead, before I can even get in the room, is Ike on the move, somehow with a great, inexplicable whoosh, and Johnny turning his chair with his feet, to face the train head-on before impact.

"Grandma, can you stop this shit!?" I plead, but Grandma is getting tiny, dwarfish, looking harder at the cardinal or robin or tufted titmouth pecking away at the old pine tree out the window, lost to the fight and with no thoughts on where exactly ol' Jimbo sleeps.

You always wonder how it will go down, your hero moment, when you walk past that alley at the moment of midnight rape, when the guy in front of you decides it's time to hijack this Boeing. Or when mushrooms come atop the pizza. Will you stand up? Will they interview you on the news after? Will anybody be able to tell about that dark stain on your pants?

"Watch your throat, Johnny!" I call, meekly, all I can muster, adolescent-like, as though my voice were about to crack.

"Fuck you, Teddy," comes a response, I can't even tell who it's from.

Now I'm moving, everything happening in slow-motion, but also far too fast. *Get in there*, a voice is saying, but it doesn't sound like Proust. *Get in there you son of a bitch!* It's the same voice as the one telling me to lunge at full velocity over a tree stump with a bag of burritos tucked under my arm like a football. *Put the shoulder pads on*, it says, the same voice telling me co-domestication is a real headache, just the worst, and that relationships are overrated, staying single the only protector. The voice I so often have to lockdown in a basement-type region: It is OJ.

I'm moving with intent, with charge, Zeppelin rising from somewhere within me, but not 'Stairway' or anything with strings or a too-long intro. My arms are swinging—*these shoulders are huge!*— and my head is lowered with wrecking ball possibility, carnage-causing, fearless, like I'm running stride-for-stride with a blocker, one with even bigger pads than me, and an even crazier bent to his gut. The bag swaying by my side impedes my hero's posture, or rather it did, because before I know it the Anderson's is on the floor, and everyone can see that I've ordered a beef.

There's a pause. Ike realizes he coiled back and disheveled the bag, and my face, caused a bloody trickle from my nose, his elbow still cocked behind him. My horseradish-slathered top bun is plopped on the carpet, out of its wrapped home, next to the pooling ice cream containers, their contents running and leaking.

"I thought you said you got ice cream," Johnny says, puzzled, like I'd been cheating on him by failing to mention the beef.

"You have a weight problem," Ike says, reverting and turning the blood flow into something, somehow, that is my fault. He's also let his guard down, and given Johnny a chance to get his own body moving, which he does, suddenly charging forward, until we're all a messy fat ball of 'Ski, me in between them with my elbows up and a stream of blood above my lip, this three-way dance of monsters splayed over custard and roast beef spilled all over the carpet.

There is another pause, then, when we spy Grandma at the front door, holding the pregame pizza box.

"YOU," she growls, shaking. "You fat fucks. I'll throw this right on the ground if you don't stop. I won't even pay for it."

"Ma, you're hysterical," Ike says.

The smell of pepperoni floats about the tiny room, and there's an acned delivery driver looking on. He seems neither shocked nor alarmed, simply like a man waiting for his twenty. She has anticipated the doorbell, sprung to life, and taken the pizza hostage in her little flabby arms, propping open the front screen door and threatening to toss the delicious Bocce's on the concrete.

She continues, oblivious to the driver. "Stop fighting. Nobody cares where Jimbo lives. Just stop." She loses her train of thought momentarily before picking up in a different place and carrying on. We all stand, slightly stunned. "And stop it, Ike. You too, Johnny. There's nobody to blame! Johnny didn't know to call 911! You all take so long in the bathroom anyways! Who would know!? And stop with the eating, all of you! It's not helping! For the love of God, look at you, Teddy." She's adamant, red in the face.

I'm not sure how it's come back on me, the pacifying hero, standing in the middle. "Me!?"

"She's right," Johnny says, and nods. "Look at you, Teddy."

"Grandma, you bitch. Can't you see I just lost a beef on weck!?"

"Teddy, the rest of you, you all have problems, and just for that…"

She can't be blamed. She thinks she is helping, thinks we'll see the error, the flatulence, even, of our ways. That we'll hug, sing "Kumbaya," get our arms around each other in those tight emotional hugs where you can smell one another's BO, and order a salad next time at Family Tree. She's bending over, tipping the box on its side, and with all seeming might, with great focused intent, she turns it upside down over the front stoop.

The three of us move forward as one, a great fat person tidal wave rushing the tiny door. The delivery driver steps back, and Grandma is smalling herself again, looking, rightfully, like she's expecting to get hit, tears running down her face. Ike has remembered his blame, his anger at Johnny, his disbelief, and, from down in his gut, shouts "Who orders a pregame pizza, anyways!? You see your bullshit? You wait till halftime!"

Maybe he's just going for a condescending head tap, but the house is too small, and they start swinging. All is lost. I'm tripping and stumbling over the hearth, horrified, just as the mozzarella starts to stick to the pavement and the driver reaches a safe distance away at the end of the yard and I realize my foot is sticking to the floor because of the horseradish under my boot heel. There are punches, and throat punches, and a great wail. The pizza guy is on his cell phone and I'm hanging onto Ike's back, Johnny down and trying to protect his face. Ike was right about it all, about us, about being from here, and his conviction seems to be extolled into the thrust of that throat punch. We're tumbling, and Helka is circling, crying, but then ducking in quick to whack Ike on the back of the head, except that is where I'm currently lodged so she misses and hits me, and I let out a "Grandma, fuck!" Johnny is laughing, or crying, I can't tell because I taste blood and the adrenaline is soaring, the police are being summoned, and it's not even time for kickoff as we roll around on the concrete alongside the pepperoni oil cups, the pizza damaged beyond all repair. A terminal case. A sad state of loss. It never had a chance.

23. CHICAGO (5-2)

It's always led to this, the thing the guy in the movie does, eventually, the hero, after his vision has left, his friends have betrayed him, his wares and sinew gone out to lunch. One of those moments where he looks at his hands and wonders where everything in them has gone, like he's never seen them so empty before, and his woman is fucking someone else, someone with an Italian sports car, a Ferrari, and tons of chest hair, and he's just found out. It's his fault, too, because he cared *too much*, tried too hard, loved too deeply, spent too much time with orphans in Tibet or Niger or wherever. It's the point, his point, his time, to do something removed, ascetic, to prove and illustrate the unfairness of the world, the indifference of society, everything stacked against him and his empty hands by a vicious God.

It's the moment of him thinking, "Fuck it. This'll show 'em."

It's still about them, though, and so not heroic at all. Real heroes go to the bathroom, say fuck it, turn the water warm and then make it red with the help of a straight razor. Or they bust their gut, literally, rupture everything, take what they want, do it and overdo it with the things that made them happy, poison everything normal and balanced and Monday-to-Friday. Spend the currency and worth of every healthy moment on the fleeting ones, the ones of grease and smoke and touchdowns, getting the soul out, boozy punctuations of the cheeks by the mouth corners.

So for now I'm only playing at the hero, and a general, resigned *fuck it* settling in is how I happen to take up Dustin's offer for work at his warehouse. I'm suddenly surrounded by big shoulders, Chicago being the city of such, after all, but now, here, in a concrete-floored and impossibly-ceilinged warehouse, it's all in my face. Real, at last, and I'm holding a something-pound roll of shrink wrap, a paper towel roll on steroids, all the colored stretchy plastic in the Midwest, its industrial-strength cardboard corrugation currently cutting into my palms as I try to wrap a pallet.

"You may want to start off with the gloves," Dustin says, with a great smile, observing my work, his arms at his sides, veins noticeably bulging, always bulging, now so evident from my 90-degree bend at the waist. There are calluses, too, on his palms, under those formidable arms, though I'm not exactly sure what a callus is, what they look like, where they go, how they spend their days.

At any rate, here it is: to X's chagrin, to her great consternation, I've begun the transition to Everyman status.

"Fuck books," I say to Dustin, smirking, feigning a smile, trying at the jovial teammate, sliding on some thick gray work gloves, my forehead dripping with an unfamiliar substance, a sort of smiley face of perspiration visibly forming in the gut region of my gray t-shirt, the mouth an O around where the belly button hides, its expression seeming to say, "Oooooohhhhh, whaaaaaaat da fack!"

"The lady says this is cool for a minute, huh?" Dustin seems concerned, like when we're out and it's right before he asks, "One more?" When he knows it's super late, and it's a Tuesday, and we maybe don't have time to get another one down before bar time. I placate, as he must know I will, and we're ordering 'nother ones, thinking ourselves clutch, and then still sneaking outside to suck down a stick before we start in on the one for the road we'll have to hurry to finish.

"The lady who?" I reply, earning guffaws, the good hearty kind, work friends now, like Jimbo and Thurman, O.J. and his blocker.

All in a day's job, as they say.

And then I'm back at it, bending at the knees—or did Dustin say to bend at the back? Or, no, is that lifting? *Lift* with the *back*, yeah, that sounds right—either way, I'm down as close to the ground while awake and sober as I've been in some years, the skin on my feet stretching like sausage casings as I pull. I try not to dwell on that metaphor, so far away from lunch.

I don't know what it is we're wrapping on these big pallets, though I envision something nefarious—cocaine, heroin, sold-off M-16s from a former Eastern Bloc country—to entice things, lend an air of importance, though that's what I've come to get away from.

Dustin has simply taken care of it all, smoothed things out with everyone around us, someone named Foreman who holds some kind of pedigree around these parts, these south side streets so industrial, vacuous, graffiti-ish, barbed wire-y, filled with longshoreman-looking types, everybody smoking and wearing dirty work pants.

"So you're giving it up? The dream?" He gives me a concerned look again, which is concerning to me now, it being too early for such gravity.

"I still got a shot to get picked in next year's draft, don't ya think?"

With this, another guffaw, another great one, from the gut, head back, aimed at the ceiling. A forklift purrs by. A muscular black guy in a flannel shirt and Timberlands walks past us and stops to give Dustin a handshake that turns into a complicated thing that keeps going and ends with Dustin's forefinger thrusting in-and-out through the glory hole the guy is forming with thumb and pointer. Dustin introduces me: "Check this out, 'nother Bills fan, bro!"

The dude gives me a once-over, shaking his head. "Shit, man, you crazy, too!?"

"Not if I stay on my meds. Which is beer."

The three of us laugh together amidst the shrink-wrapped pallets and the shit-talking and the fluorescent glow and that weird kind of working-class humanity I'm trying to elbow my way into, Proust be damned.

"Well," Proust says now, snidely, pronouncedly French, "you seem a ways from your computer, from the rhythm, from the magic."

There's a pallet jack nearby in desperate need of some WD-40. I use the high squeak to pretend I can't hear him.

Aside from the stinging pain creeping up my forearm toward the butt of my elbow, a region and muscle I'd never been quite aware

162

of and thus had previously taken for granted; and despite this being Hour Two, though I'm swearing off looking at the clock, lest I see how it creeps, snail-like; and despite the gray under and around me, the concrete, the sadness; and despite the tough guy fuckery I'm going to have to go through just to complete Day One intact, unstrained, unbroken; and despite everyone laughing at me, probably—I can feel it—because it's remedial work and I somehow still don't know what I'm doing or even have the right shoes; and despite the feeling that my gut is too pronounced, Jello jiggly when I have to move, and the neon lights so shrill to my hangover, and the sense, back there somewhere behind my heart, that poetry is being lost (Proust, pleading, crying, arms at his side, hands up at the wrist, desperate: "But this isn't *trying*." Me, wanting to hurt him: "You ever even get a callus, you Frenchy fuck?"): even now, as I sweat, and it feels bayou-ish from the grundle to the armpit, and last night's beer is causing an increasing ache in the temples, I actually feel pretty good. I'm taking a look around, and there's a UPS guy over there, smiling as Dustin signs his handheld computer contraption that symbolizes movement, progress. There's a vending machine with some jalapeno cheddar Cheetos I've been eye-chomping with each pass. There are some guys I could talk football with, certainly, once I catch my breath. *Relax, let's just get this shit done.* And then to the couch afterward, or to the bar, we'll have a cold one, and another, and yuck it up like chesty fellas with big arms at the kind of neon beer sign place where an old barmaid knows us, breaks our balls, gets us yet another with her stained-teeth laugh, as we shit-talk wives, bosses, fiancés.

There's an absence of dreaminess here. A matter-of-fact life that could be gone towards, appreciated, just turn the head gears down a bit, stick a broom handle in that mind crank, stop the interminable spinning. You can work hard, go home, crack a Budweiser can, get some baseball on the TV. I could get into caring about baseball. Batting averages, spitting. Or not, also, just sit there and slurp and stare, placated by the lights, the perceived manliness, the only thoughts being on the beer can count and what's for dinner.

Of course, like every pseudo-hero, there's always the back-of-the-dome dream. The inkling, still there, the root impossible to wipe out, that one day, back strained, lost amidst the Everyman customs and blue collar rigmarole, amidst the simplicity and the newfound ease of it all, there's still a chance for it to happen. The hero turns, rising from his knees and the great Sisyphean task, and there she will be, having seen the error of her ways, having suddenly realized his great, delicate genius, his soft way but robust character, the beauty of his subtle chivalry. Despite his vast collection of failures and paunchy gut, and the fact she wanted to fuck Mario from Sales, she'll remember the sensitivity, how he introduced her to Fellini, and to that taco joint that wasn't even on Yelp. She'll want him back, and he'll say no. The dream: a chance to flip her off with gruff sarcastic laughs, turn his back with a chorus of bellows from his fellows around him, at his back, his posse—his pride remaining intact, true, the victor after all.

As it is with certain heady types, those who went to college and tried caring about politics or critical human thought, who developed certain sensitive-leaning idiosyncrasies helpful for scoring with certain kinds of chicks *and* for using as an excuse as to why you couldn't score with more chicks, this vindication, this from-the-rooftops shout, takes the form of Publication, with a capital P. The ultimate *Fuck You*. The validation. "Ma, you're fat son ain't such a layabout after all, eh!? Eh!?" The chance to say, "This time, the tacos is on me!" So, the dream: a chance to know, to feel, even before the diagnosis, "Ok, I can die now."

Maybe after I've been here for a bit, have a whole glut of blue collar buds whose respect I've come to earn with my steady resilience, a gamut of friends who I watch games with, who I bullshit with; when I'm so in the groove with the ridiculously oversized cellophane wrap and the pallet jacks, and I have my own work gloves and tough boots that don't look new, right when I stop caring, there it will be, with a BOOM. Or is it a BAM? Suddenly strutting, out of nowhere Funkadelic—or is it Parliament?—hits heavy as I check my phone, and everything is all groove and gangster swagger lean, sunglasses materializing out of nowhere on my face. The good news, spiritual substantiation, one *Yes* from one email from some New York asshole who doesn't even really care. Capital S Success, the reason for which phone calls are made, schedules cleared, book tours planned and jobs quit. *This has been fun and all, fellas, but c'mon,* and the Meters count off into an earned *Aiiiii-YAH*. Giddy momentum plucks itself from the rote. Mom gets all teary and proud. X takes me out for rewarding pizza. Father smiles from on high, lighting the celebratory cigar he never had. Ike buys me a bottle, Helka cooks roast beef, bursting with pride over the hot stove, and Johnny shakes his head in disbelief. Everyone looks at me a bit different, everyone looks.

Proust, even, seems in awe.

"I always knew this day would come for you, my friend."

"You never liked my shit, so fuck you."

"It's not that I didn't like it."

"It's that you didn't read it."

"Two completely different things."

"You got me there, you bastard!"

I'll take a hit from his cigarette, in one of those holder things, and we'll clasp each other's backs and walk off into the night toward a pub where we'll drink too much and pound the table with our fists and laugh too loud about the sad beauty of having it all figured the fuck out.

Except I've avoided such dreaminess, not really thinking at all, not even thinking about the Bills, Dustin and I having collectively, subconsciously, deciding not to curse it, not to ruin the good luck they've had against bad teams. Not knowing anyways how to discuss the off feeling, that strangeness to us, that of a mid-season opportunity, of being in some kind of hunt.

Oh my god that stiff arm!

Shh, shhhh. (Looking around, and up, as if someone might hear).

Just waiting for that other shoe, the flag thrown after the big play. Something. Just don't, just *shhhhh*.

Even now, as we're standing in the sun after Dustin has declared "Smoke time!" and I feel I've earned it, stretching my arms out to the concrete jungle around us. Nothing's bad, and nothing is really being spoken. Tender silence between old allies. Smoke plumes blowing around, the only thing missing some beers. A whiff of awkwardness settles, from our reckoning—does he see it, too?—of a relationship so out-of-context.

And then we have to go back in. There won't be beers, but there'll be another hour of bending and such, and no couches or stools, and that's just before lunch. My right palm is bleeding from the pre-glove attempt, I'm dabbing the side of my jeans, trying to not let anyone see, and there's suddenly a knot in my neck. Plus, there's that thing where a cigarette feels like a good idea, and all is right, and it's a communal fraternal moment of stepping outside, stopping what you're doing, and you can't wait, can't believe how good of an idea it was, can't believe it wasn't your idea, especially good when at work, an escape. But when you've had too much the night before, and it's still the AM, it can come on suddenly, and you become at once conscious of the interstitial fluid in your brain, feel a bit short of breath, full of fatigued loathing. There's a mix of toothpaste now with the smoke, and sun obnoxiousness. At once I realize it's only Tuesday—or, actually, tomorrow, tomorrow is only Tuesday. And there's the familiar weekday feel that I should have studied something else, came in to different parents, been born somewhere else, joined the Peace Corps, swallowed some serotonin pills upon waking.

"One thing, bro…" Dustin says, holding the door for me.

"Anything." *Tell me anything you want that I can do for you. Anything. You need a place to crash? You wanna get outta here and do some daytime drinking? Want me to try to get you some crack? No, no crack, sure, joking, ridiculous, but, yeah, let's do it, anything.*

"You gotta get here a bit earlier tomorrow."

And that's it, it won't be long now: to saddle up, swallow the pride, send another one-last-email to the editor; second, third check those manuscript queries; follow-up with the assholes, the big city pricks holding all my pages of magical prose, my boys, my pride, sitting there sad and crowded atop big oak, pine, whatever desks. In midtown, in downtown, some are already in the backs of trucks making their way across some historically-named bridge to a dump in Queens, or a recycling joint in Jersey. If I could just give 'em all a quick nudge, have those stiffs in ties shuffle some papers, have them lean forward and take their feet off their desk—always with the legs up on the desks! Just email and remind them and they'll bolt forward and bat their forehead with a palm, "Ah, yes, yes, fuck, of course, yes! Rawski! The New Orleans tale! The one with real heart and almost no cliché. That was something! Magic. The lyricism! Really glad I got a 3rd email from that Midwestern freelance writer whom I've never heard of…"

For I have given it a go, the Everymanning, the old university try, as they say. It was a good ride, today, these couple hours. At least I could tell 'em all, everyone who asks, "Yeah, it's hard down there at the dock."

"I thought it was a warehouse."

"Yeah…Times are indeed hard."

"How much time you put in, you say?"

Enough to say fuck it and leave. And like that, again, for real, it's time to call Grandma. Dustin has refused me, in not so many words, with this subtle insistence on work, effort, alarm clockery.

It won't be long before X rebukes me, too, before she upends my hero card simply by already being there, by never going away. She can never play a part in the movie if she won't leave. She doesn't want to fuck Mario from Sales, she wants to fuck me, but only after I've worked all day in an office, after I've shaved my sideburns and learned to tie a tie.

Tie a tie—how redundant.

For now though, there's just enough in the bank, Pilsen is near, and it's time for tacos. Some *cochinita*, some *carnitas*, but after that it's time to eat myself beyond stuffed. Those Cheetos won't get it done, not all the Cheetos in all the vending machines in all of industrial southside Chicago. First, tacos, and then on with the suicide. It's time to bust the gut, hero-style—heroes aren't born, they are marinated and braised and poked with holes that are stuffed with garlic and sizzled on a very hot flattop, then doused with salsa and bits of onion and cilantro. It's a process. There are the Grandma-given 20s and the chicken wings of Buffalo, futilely floating manuscripts and story pitches and half-stabs at adulthood, all of it to be sent up in clean, aromatic plumes of smoke, cooking smoke. The legacy-concreting, hero-making time seems at hand.

24. LA NOVA PIZZERIA
371 West Ferry
Buffalo, NY 14213

Somebody tried to rob the place once. It makes sense: the neighborhood is a bad one, and one of those bad ones that becomes bad suddenly, like all the houses collectively decided to jump into a pool and the only way to get in comfortably was all at once, and once they were in, they were all the way in. At that point, any given individual might as well hop out, do a backflip or a cannonball, splash the dry sunbathers, disrupt the peace, laugh it up, create discomfort, be some kind of summertime hero and shout, "I was here, fuckers!" Step up. Be somebody.

And so, businesses get robbed.

The neighborhood announces itself, underlines other-side-of-the-tracks clichés as soon as you turn off Delaware. Go three blocks down West Ferry, then, past some moderately decaying Victorians that you can't quite be sure about, through and around a turnabout—"Go to the right," Helka would remind you, three times, if she were here, which she wouldn't be, because of the neighborhood—and you'll find yourself a couple blocks away from where you were but now off, perturbed, a bit self-conscious and double-checking the door lock. You're at once in the middle of the degradation of the city you've long heard about at airport bars and from cab drivers, over a decade's worth of negative headlines and unemployment stats. The decay, the rusting of American dreamscapes, the peeling paint and siding and saggy-ass porches. The people who live over here sit out on their stoops, even if there are no stoops to sit on, some setting out plastic chairs to watch you go by with some sort of hatred in their eyes, or so you imagine, sitting there so naked in your grandmother's car with its Tonawanda dealership license plate holder, her money in your pocket and your Bills hat on, but that last part doesn't matter.

I like to bring Ike or Johnny. Muscle. Or, really, fat. A bit of each, I guess, rolled together into an indeterminate ball that sits on the passenger seat and makes you look at least a bit less timid. Helps you laugh and look around this 'hood where robberies happen, with rapes on the regular, according to Grandma, who peruses the headlines and the six o'clock news seemingly only for such info. The bad stuff being her validation, "Oh, you see? You see, Teddy!? I told you you should never leave the goddamn house!"

The thing is, La Nova is a bit different, and if you can get your boots in the door without any unwanted aggression, penetration, if you can leave the motor running and Ike or Johnny in the seat smoking, seeming like they're keeping an eye on things, like they even got your back, you shouldn't have a problem. Once inside, with the bustle of the counter orders and the delivery drivers coming and going, you realize you're safe, ensconced. The guy behind the counter with all the curly chest hair—chest hair on his forearms, even—has your back, too. It's at once capital-F Family, the *Old Country* kind, a slow montage of hearty hugs in a house-stuffed familial holiday time reunion. A simple *Howyadoin'* letting you know how you're doing, that you are alright. And you realize, feel and smell it at once, with the oven heat wafts, the pepperoni's crisping and cupping, palming their own grease, wings growing lascivious in a hot oil bath.

But then again, everyone is just trying to be somebody. To spend what's there while there's time on the clock, or some sports metaphor about a warning, two minutes, what-have-you. There is always the lone gunman, the John Wayne, or one of those rappers that's always pointing at the camera and kind of cocking his head to the side and constantly questioning, "What?!?" I feel bad for the guy that walked in here, armed, and ended up being chased, shot, killed as he tried to scale a fence while toting a backpack full of mafia pizza dough. He must've had no idea, never seen a single DeNiro flick.

As I recall the story, walking in the door, completing my journey for big barbecue wings, fried, sauced, then quick-grilled, just for the black mark, a nominal caramelization a Proust-type might speak of, so far away from the familiar bars, with their yoga pants and short walks home, comfort and neighborhood ease and accessibility, I can't help but flash on Dustin's viewpoint, his latest newfound philosophy, coming from books and a nascent interest in literature. Also, from a gentle elbow nudging from me, his teacher, who gets more ear than he deserves. But he got here mostly on his own: everyone stop with the dreaming, with the expectation, with the center of the universe-ing.

"Kids, third grade or so, just start 'em in with Cormac McCarthy. The dark stuff. The Lottery and that shit. Help 'em with the long sentences, sure, don't be ridiculous, but, just, ya know—isn't it enough just to exist? Everybody's gotta dream, and have their dreams nurtured, stroked, the whole *you can be whatever you wannabe* poison. Bullshit. Just live. Don't die. Enjoy it. Pay rent. Who's special? You're not so special. Look at you, Teddy. Even you, you're not so special."

At that, we guffawed, wide-eyed, late-night knowing, more real and less insulting, no indictment but the one on civilization for not getting it. We could cheers to that.

Although if I *were* to get killed on my way for some grub, the story therein, what it would do for the manuscript, and for X. For her to collect my little savings, and be interviewed back home, by the Reader or something. It would be one of those cover stories with a picture where she's sitting on the couch holding a copy of the New Orleans book, its cover done by someone awesome, minimalist or some such artistic term, the trade paperback by Random House, tight and neat, like a Roth, my name big and bold. There'd be a picture of me in a frame behind her, looking stoic in black-and-white, standing by the Golden Gate maybe, the sad and tortured poet cut down on a quest for his second favorite pizza. The sales would go toward her new condo, sure, but then there'd be so much she'd have to set up a fund, an education type thing, going to an impoverished, underprivileged aspiring young food writer from Chicago's south side. A girl named Latisha from 47th and Halsted, with simple but huge dreams of thinking of new words and ways to capture the essence of roasted garlic. To bring it to life for legions of hungry readers, the devourers of calorie-poetics.

Once inside La Nova, with the smell, the Bocce's-leaning crust, there's a sense of belonging, a new one, that fresh, weird adult thing of bad neighborhoods and outsider-dom. When you can get over the airplane sweat, throw yourself in, venture forth in a strange city on a new night and open the door to a bar that looks off, sketchy. Go to Harlem, the Ninth Ward, Detroit, and have an experience, before you become hunched over and triple-check your locks at night, believing everything on the news like it was scripture.

The Caputi's waitress, her yoga pants, seems so far away in suburban insularity. Though here I start to pity her, almost, like she did me, a bit, when I drank-and-divulged last night. I probably said too much, about X's disappointment in life, and in me, in my gut and my seeming inability to procure a condo. I told her about the ulcer, too, as she washed the pint glasses, how it could kill me, and I tried to hint at the romanticism therein. Then I told her about my father taking his own life after the Super Bowl, and in a joking, see-how-strong-I-am aside, said, "You probably weren't even born for that Super Bowl!" *Har har.*

"I was 2," she said, her face turning from puppy dog-ish to poker, as if I'd insulted her existence. I had imagined her clitoris warming, or whatever it does, but then she just drummed a finger on the bar, kind of looking off over my shoulder, even as "Whiter Shade of Pale" hit and it should have been our time, our eye contact time, our slow-motion slow-pan scene where she tells me it'll be alright and then pauses, as if remembering something, and in hushed, conspiratorial tones whispers, "You wanna get out of here?" But really she was biding, being polite, making sure to pay her dues and show enough cleavage and some semblance of a smile to ensure that I would spend it all. Which I did.

Out here on Buffalo's sad west side, as I ponder a bartender who wears tight pants and will never love me, no matter how I tip, is perspective. The old saying, how you can't go to your house again, or the other way around, whatever it is. What does that even mean? Helka tells me *all the time* I can and should come home. Either way, it feels good to know you can't change who you are. At the very least, with the mafia ties and the crumbling neighborhood and all the pepperoni and pillowy pan crust and the way the wing barbecue sauce coalesces into the blue cheese once you get out of here and back to a happy coffee table, after you've faced the fear and risked it all for a pickup, after you've lived some life, it's good to know you can't put yoga pants on La Nova.

25. BUFFALO (7-9)

I'm in Helka's backyard, phone in my neck nook, smoking under an eave, watching a falling snow, one of volume and density, billow down on the empty grass. The flakes take their time falling, some mixing with plumes of my Camel as I shiver in a flannel shirt and look up, toward God, unable to see him, my eyes just filling with wetness instead.

"What we could really use is something about patios," the editor says through the line.

"Patios? When did this become an outdoor magazine?"

"Well, Ted, I'm just not sure there's enough traffic for Buffalo, or for chicken wings."

"Oh, I think there'll be traffic. And it's actually really about the pepperoni, the way it curls up and…"

"Sure, sure, sure, but, see, Teddy, we need a list for the spring preview issue. It's going to be very list-forward, and people love checking out new patios."

"List-forward?"

"That's right. You know, for when it gets warmer."

"Who says it's going to get warmer?"

It's been mostly inevitable, like these flakes spewing down, like the larger number on the wrong side of the Bill's two-digit W-L record, the phrase sports fans know best surmises a season. A full year of sweat, toil, getting up early, really early, to stretch and take showers with large groups of guys, then leaning forward and putting your shoulder into it, doing something hard. It's reduced, later, to those three words, spoken like one, *sevenandnine*, and that's the whole story. One of failure, in this case. Shortcoming. Clitorises left dry. I take it like Helka takes her validation from the evening news, *of course, humanity is fucked, nobody cares, down the tubes, why try?* With a touch of the indignant, too, *Oh really? Fuck me I guess, huh.*

Fuck me? I don't care anyhow. I'm a man, with a smirk and a smoke, have it your own ignorant way. Suddenly I have an Italian accent and cocked shoulders, and I'm wagging my finger. A bit of victimhood, as well, chin up, eyes wide, hands to the side in consternation, *do you see now how completely mad the world is?*

"You know, Ted, we work ahead," the editor goes on, "and I know you're there, but I'd need you back here and on-board for this one."

"Proust never wrote about any goddamn patios," I mutter.

"What's that?"

"Proust. Nevermind. You wouldn't get it. French lit."

"Ted, do you know I have a Master's in French Literature?"

I had forgotten, or never knew, I don't know which. Maybe we could have been friends, had I ever read any Proust, and as a result he'd have put me in touch with other editors after we'd polished Manhattans at some low-lit bar with booths along the wall, where dreamy-eyed old journalism types talked of the truth, and all the sentences they'd had cut, but still got up that very morning to write it all, to right it all, and then get drunk again. I could have been one of those names that you see here and then see there, and there's an associated bio that lists multiple publications you've actually heard of, one of those writers that collects by-lines like, well, people who collect things. Things to put on the mantle, next to the candles. Pride to put in the bank, pride that swells every time I sit back in my chair and sigh deeply and nod privately to myself before taking a big drink, one I earned.

Masters? Well, that's why you're the boss.

No, I'm the boss because your sentences are too damned long.

"Speaking of which, how is that novel coming?" He asks this as though speaking to a child in need of weaning, or who is teething, doing something to be gotten over. *How is that rash?* Something to be up and saddled and mounted and done with. Broken, like a wild horse. Made a bitch, like I would be in prison maybe, knocked down to my rightful place in the pecking order of the world's endless, malicious indifference.

"The novel?"

"How's it coming?" I can see him leaning back, putting his feet up on the desk, a grin on his face, condescending, enjoying it, bald and bespectacled and full on his Masters, like every editor.

"How's it coming?"

"Yeah, how's it coming?"

"It came already. Premature ejaculation. Always my problem."

There seem to be few points left to make. The closing chapters, the truthful ones, of resolution and philosophy decided-upon, where friends come together again. The shits have been taken, the lessons learned. The French word that starts with D that I can never remember or pronounce, where the hero has been found, made whole, earned his scars, chosen or been denied his spoils, banged the broad everyone knew from first eyelash bat was The One. But now there's no more roasted garlic to riff on, not much left of the book: the season's over and there are no clitorises at my doorstep. Nothing left of the Bills, or of my time here.

In fact, there's nobody left at all, no one but Helka and I. Johnny and Ike and their big-gutted existences dissolved into a conflicted mess of airport departures and avoidances and, "Yeah, I'll see ya," Helka looking on with tears creeping into her eyes and awkward hugs where you don't look at each other before or after, tightness to it, but forced. Calls made about Johnny, calls made about Ike. Flights checked on and, thankfully, eventually, taken off, surging up and through the air and snow and out of the orbit of Mighty Taco and bad coffee and the old lady smell about Grandma's house.

I think about a time in the future when the three of us will be emptying out this very house, hating each other for our very presences, the way they don't allow for tears, and hating ourselves individually, for not doing more when she was alive to render those tears unnecessary. Survivor's guilt, like Norwood had, hopefully.

I've been shrugging about such and ignoring Mom's incessant need to dissect, psychologize, recap the battle. I've been reclining and licking my own wounds, looking at the framed picture of O.G. Johnny and shrugging, telling him, truthfully, "I don't know." And, also, "Playoffs next year, for sure. One last hurrah for Jackson, at least. C'mon Freddie…one more year, right?" O.G. would say something like, "Don't blame Norwood," to which I'd reply, "No, I blame myself," and then I'd have to change the subject before the tears started, something lighter, something like, "So your sons were both assholes, huh?"

Har har.

Aside from the familial scabs and scars, I've also, today, for lunch, been licking the horseradish from the outer edges of my beef as Helka goes at her Anderson's ice cream—"Whatever, on a cone," actually part of my order—and pretends there was no Middle East-type throwdown in this very room just days ago. As long as the editor thing is happening, while the end is approaching, the pages in the right hand receding in volume, all the promise flipping toward the front of the binding, and the resignations have been tendered, there is another call left to be made, I know. We've been ducking each other, my story one of gritty work combined with family time, hard to penetrate, even for a fiancé, while hers was something more legitimate, I'm sure. Searching around Chicago, perhaps, for a place to keep her bed and all accrued possessions in a manner allowing her to present them stylishly; or even, maybe, looking for a less fat, more interested person with which to share said presentation. The streets and possibilities are many there, for both.

There's been a newfound chilliness coming in with the cold air, but this must be dealt with. After lunch, and upon retrieving another mug of coffee from Helka's kitchen—where she sits, in a robe, under an afghan, having just puttered back from the thermostat, ice cream finished, watching TV and waiting for me to make a decision about dinner—I fire up another Camel and head back outside.

"Are you still mad about the Tim Kelly thing?" X asks. I hadn't realized it'd been chewing away at me these past few months, nor that she could tell. The little slip that broke the camel's back, as they say. But who am I, the non-attainer of a condo, to judge?

After a beat, long enough for a sip of the hot stuff from an old cracked mug and a drag from the Camel, blowing smoke out over Tonawanda, into the swirling snow, I say, "No, baby. I'm not mad about anything."

"It's just that you always put the Comeback Game on, and he doesn't play in it."

She's right, of course, and with this acknowledgement comes the kind of awkward silence that ends most phone conversations, that can be used, amplified, into something bigger, if one has fucked up in such a way, has vacated to such a degree, has gone all the way to Buffalo, and stayed, for reasons never really clarified.

"Maybe we should've watched the Super Bowl tape instead?" she asks, searching.

"Maybe. Well, no. Probably not." I feel tears of my own welling, and she doesn't know but there's a tenderness, reluctance, around every goodbye, even if it's one you've been anticipating.

"No?"

"Maybe some O.J."

"I'd really like that."

"I'd like that, too."

I think back to when we first met. She thought it was all so cute. She thought the Bills hat was probably something I didn't normally wear out to a semi-classy bar in Logan Square with craft cocktails on a Saturday night. I'd just gotten a job—freelancing, but still, a job, and just out of, okay, *sort of just out of* college. She even knew the name of the rag, and seemed mildly impressed. I wasn't looking too fat, and hinted gently at the tortured brooder, the tender poet, lying just beneath this bit of flab and fandom. An inauspicious start, but one with promise, and I bought her another tequila thing that came in a chalice with a vaguely Latin name. She went over her history, Skokie and a fancy-but-not-too-fancy college. I listened, and she listened, accepting enough about Kerouac and yielding a mild enthusiasm about trying a new pizza place.

It was enough to get us to a point where it's years later and we're waiting around, maybe for something better, maybe for it to get better, more like what seemed to be happening all around us. Buying a ring, eventually, because it was impossible to forget the next suggested sacrament, as every weekend became lousy with weddings, the Save the Dates piling up on the refrigerator, arguing with one another, clamoring for future days of forced happiness and open—hopefully—bars. I even forced myself through an awkward one-knee proposal, a memory that haunts, if only because of the look in her eye, like when the appetizer comes out, and it sounded so good on paper, but then, tableside, you think, *wasn't this supposed to be fried?* Then there were all those houses being purchased, which later became houses with babies inside.

There she was, frustrated at her career, focusing on it more, as if further dedication could lessen her frustration. Middle age settling early on the heart, the dissatisfaction coming out in weird ways, aggressive ways, like scoffing and steadfastly refusing to try a newfound taco stand in Little Village. An increased denial of sex, too, more "you're just drunk and grabby" excuses. And there I was, letting myself go, putting less and less time in on the book, more effort needed to care, my gut growing bigger, more grumbly. Between this, and us, was a trip to a doctor. A simple flare up, but one deemed "something to keep an eye on," the doctor looking down at his clipboard of doom as I thought of certain tragic ends, knowing I should never have agreed to a check-up. I had taken it as something that might end this wheel-spinning, this lonely keyboard knuckle-dragging, this sad Bills viewing and emotional overeating. I'd tried a fatalistic recklessness on, then purchased it and wore it every day. It seasoned everything, my meals most of all, as the time between them grew shorter and the dollar amounts spent larger.

"How'd we get to this?" she wonders. "It's like the Spoilers!"

"The Oilers, baby. The team was the Oilers."

"Why would they name a team that? They're like frackers? Proud frackers?"

"Bunch o' rapists down in Texas, you know that."

"Well, is there any chance for our comeback?" She probably grins saying this, despite herself, always proud to slip in an *aww shucks* sports reference.

"That performance will never be repeated."

"You always said that."

"Yeah. I'm sorry. I'm sorry for all the things I always said, or, well, say." Trying to make it hurt, but I mean it, too, and I'm not sure which one more.

"Over and over you go," she says, trailing off. But then, as if something occurred to her, as if another shoe was dropping, she adds, "But that's ok. You know, maybe you're better there."

Maybe I'm no good anywhere. But I don't say this, only think of it later, like a screenplay I'd like to get back to one day. Here, now, I just stare up over the roof at the gray sky and take another sip of coffee, snow beginning to land in the mug.

With these pages receding, not much of the book left, there are so many other calls that still need to be made, so many characters to be seen to again. Not like life, where most everyone drifts away or drops out of view over the mind's horizon, where perspective and intuition tell you they're doing something else, something noble, something grand, with a family and a big house—one step up on a condo, even. I think on them, thinking on me, looking back and laughing. Except there aren't nobler things. There are houses, but it's all grass-cutting and saving to get a new roof, basements to get finished one day, the rigmarole of dentist appointments and waiting rooms at dentist offices and having to go to a separate, pediatric dentist and sit and try to smile at the other yawning parents pretending at maturity, hoping for salvation in a new electric toothbrush. Everybody forgets about you, about me, about that laugh, about the hushed agreement that brought glasses to clink together in a dark corner one night.

I think of Mom by the fire, maybe thinking of Dad but probably not, mostly just wondering why we all can't get along, can't get over a silly game played so long ago. A game that cost us everything, if we're being mopey about it, which, as the gravity of near-end chapters necessitates, we must now be. I think of Ike and Johnny, both off on a plane, always on those planes, forever jetting somewhere in my mind's eye. I think of Smoke and Dustin, maybe waiting, maybe forgetting, maybe not even caring, with their beer and their plights, which I don't know if I help either shoulder. I think of the Caputi's vixen and how we never took that ride. I think of everybody who's ever starred, even briefly, in an uncredited role, in this little movie of mine. They all play like a montage, and now here's Jackson, and Norwood, too, and Fitz, fucking Fitz, with his stupid face and inability to not break hearts, to let us break even, and wow, look at that, even O.J., with all that baggage, all that drama. I think of the real estate agent, whom I should call back, but if I did, and I was honest, she would merely laugh.

I think of Teressa.

"I wish things would have been better for you," I tell her.

"Oh, I had my fun."

"You must hate chicken wings."

"We can't control what defines us." She tries to force a smile but there's a tear in the corner of her eyes.

"Well, I really like your chicken wings."

"Oh, thanks for that, Toddy." She blushes a bit, holding her chin up.

"It's Teddy."

"Right. Ted. How silly. I'm not used to being out here with the people."

"You know, a woman's place isn't really in the kitchen. I'm actually quite progressive. Quite woman-forward."

"Look at you, a gentleman. A true gentleman, and such a strong young thing, too."

"Some of that is actually fat, but thanks."

"Ya know what I'd like to do for you?"

"Make me something to eat?"

"I want to make you something to eat." We both laugh and I don't know how I did it while being polite, how I steered the conversation just right, but now she's shuffling off toward the back kitchen and I'm leaning over the bar, grabbing myself a cold one, and all is right and I haven't fucked anything up.

Later, as I lay in bed, staring at the ceiling, my stomach doing a bit of post-Mighty Taco gurgling, sloshing and protesting, trombone-playing (this being my big dinner decision, and it being met with, "Again? Teddy, you're gonna turn into a Mighty Taco," and me replying, "That sounds nice," and promising soberly that this would be my last time, and her shuffling, tiny step by tiny step, her feet never really lifting from the carpet, down the hallway for an envelope and a cash wad), I'm thinking I should get up, sit on the toilet, crack the window, and blow smoke out into the Tonawanda night. But first I drop an old friend a line.

"Proust, I'm sorry."

"I'm sorry, too."

"For what? I shouldn't have insulted you like that. I'll be honest, I've never read anything you wrote."

"Same here, Teddy. I never cared much for your style."

"Well, I didn't even try with you."

"It's fine."

"No, it's not. I'm nothing. You're great. Timeless. Classic. Literary moist clitori all around!"

He takes a moment to think on this. "What does that mean?"

"It means that your mom was proud of you."

"Is that what this is about, Teddy?"

"I think so. I pretend I don't care, but I really just fantasize about Mom telling her friends, 'Teddy's a *writer*.'"

"I bet your mom's proud of you, Teddy."

"No she isn't. She just wants me to get a condo."

"You didn't let me finish. I bet your mom's proud of you," he waits a beat, "and how much pizza you can eat."

I pause at that, a smile birthing itself. "Yeah, I can really put away some pizza."

With that, I'm up and moving, the conversation lending inspiration. I'll skip taking that shit, put it on hold, stick a cork in it, as they always say about just such things, and now it's that moment in the movie where Tom Petty plays, where it's acoustic and you start to really root for this poor bastard. Who knows, maybe they'll play highlights from the Comeback Game, and they'll get the wing skin just right, on a flat, it being the best when you can take a bite from the end and then push through the loose between-bone meat with your middle finger and there's still some blue cheese from the first dunk, and at least I can have some calories and alcohol while continuing my interior dialogues. I'm out the door and on my way for a drink, and for moments of concession, for telling everybody how sorry I am how everything turned out. How it wasn't their fault, even if it was. We feel the need to say that, and you have to dial in for these talks, get your elbows some wood to rest on and let your hands fold on top of one another on the bar, a cold one in front of you and food on the way from the magical back of house. Another joint's always down the street, but this is the place, Caputi's, for comfort, for everything adult and difficult to be sorted and reconciled, while I stare at the bartender's ass and Grandma waits, sleeps, back home in her nightgown.

Once seated, a sweating Molson at hand, I watch her turn to tend to another late-night patron and remember there's a bit of a clerical matter to rectify.

In my mind, I dial up Jimbo.

"Where do you even live, Jimbo?" I ask, getting right to it. "It's still Orchard Park, right? We came a-looking..." I lean in a bit, hungry, needing to know, to hear it from him, and for the validation of my roots to echo with vehement reverberations.

"Motherfucker," he laughs, "I live in Miami."

I gasp. "Jimboooooo..."

"Why in fuck would I stick around Buffalo?"

26. CHICAGO (Offseason. Spring-ish.)

The thing to get here, what they do, is sopressata. A fantastic word, one to be repeated, to be chanted, to be turned into some kind of mantra, Sopressaaaaataaaaaa. Leave it to the Italians to make a paper-thin meat this salty and spicy, a kind of nitrate affront, a bitchslap to pepperoni, and to any and all other pizza toppings, and to get as many vowels into the backend of the label as possible. The way it rolls off the tongue, a lip-smacking onomatopoeia. I wonder, but know, how the theoretical pepperoni-carver at Bocce's would feel about me sitting here, in Chicago, on a patio in spring—spring-*ish*, anyway—just off of Fullerton, in another realm of yoga pants and little dogs and young ladies with no double chins. They walk around with their heads high, too, as if to pronounce it, to say, "See how I have no neck fat?"

It did get warmer after all, and I think, briefly, that this is not the first time I've been wrong. But the editor, with the glasses and the four-eyed ego, accepted me back, my humble late-night help, and Grandma released me finally from those flabby arms sticking out of her nightgown.

Just before our final adieu, once the snow swirls eased and after the flight arrangements were made, Helka even white-knuckled the short ride through the big, well, medium, well, small, city, to drop me off at the airport. But first, at her kitchen table, we shared a final meal.

"Don't wait till I die to come back to Buffalo," she told me.

"Don't wait till I come back to Buffalo to die," I responded.

"Oh, Teddy…"

"Just kidding, Grandma. You can die whenever you damn well please."

And with that, and her near spit take of milk, we broke up, me loving and happy, easy, alone, gazing over my burrito, across the kitchen table—the gravity of last meals requiring movement away from the couch, and from *Cheers*—at my father's mother, Helka smiling bright, like she used to, unfettered again, steering a chicken fajita into her mouth. I made a note to not get too drunk that night so I could remember her like this, taking the abuse, the ribbing, the Big Sleep discussion head-on. She wore it well, gallows humor I can only pretend at, barely, during turbulent flights, hand and voice shaky, needing a drink. Chicken driblets down her nightgown, her family left for far-flung destinations, her husband dead, her house small, and yet somehow poetry remained, the kind I still spend nights driving, drinking toward, the kind I still can't claim.

Now, back in Chicago, I share the table with a fattish man, his facial hair prematurely graying and a cold, tall Peroni on the table in front of him, both of them sweating and hinting at the simple glory of outdoor drinking days to come. Each glistens in a sun that can't make up its mind, can't fully commit one way or another to a season, but the important thing is that there is another pizza on the way for Smoke and I, us tough guys staring each other down over the last slice of the spicy pie while the theme of *The Good, the Bad and The Ugly* seems to play. Greater still, my stomach and all its woe has been sated by some Pepto.

Early April is almost patio weather in Chicago, the people over-eager to get back outside, and outdoorsy types taking in their old drinking spots now with plastic chairs and space heaters and al fresco dining. I'm absorbing it all—the early hordes emerging out of hibernation—Turkel style, or so I think, making notes in my mind, and that seems such a perfect way to put it:

Early April is almost patio weather in Chicago.

I see myself hunched, late at night, a cigarette smoldering in the ashtray next to me, face scowling over a typewriter, the whole scene in black-and-white, me getting it down with all pertinent po-etry before furrowing my brow and saying something like, "Aaahhhh…", and ripping the almost-blank page from the ribbon and tossing it at the garbage, missing the basket, the new crumpled bit laying next to other, older crumpled bits, and I stand up, hands on hips, for a few angry puffs on the smoke, frustrated, punching the wall, lighting another smoke before leaning back in, smirking to myself, everyone can see it plainly—no, yes, now that's right:

It's April, which means it's almost patio time in Chicago.

Brilliant. Just right.

I'm lost in this heroic image of myself, can feel audiences moved—*see how he shouldered through the obstacles of life?*—as can happen with such assignments, and I barely notice that the waitress has asked Smoke to snub out his smoke, and he's getting agitated. There is a white-sauced pie on the way now, as well—for journalistic integrity and all that.

"Can't smoke on a patio," he says, disgusted. "Everything's fucking changing. The other day I heard the Bills might actually be good next season. You believe that?"

I'm nodding in agreement, the subject of transience reminding me of my slant toward 30, now just weeks away, the plane making final approach. I had never thought, not in my prepubescent days of promise, nor the acned period that followed, nor the hazy college halo, that I'd still need to get off of Mom's couch when the day, decade, finally arrived. But that's where I've been since returning from Buffalo. In the basement, watching reruns, *Cheers*, my Camels making the room smell like it used to, like it can after a long Christmas vacation when Johnny's around and we get to scotching and yuletide nostalgia. Now, though, there is the patio idea, the Dylan Thomas-ish line about spring time coming back, about rebirth and what not, and I feel an itch, feel myself leaning forward. I will be paid, and then, in earnest, the scan will begin for an apartment. The south side, this time, with fresh beginnings, new horizons, taquerias for days, getting off of Mom's couch so that I may find a couch of my own to recline upon. So that I can retrieve the cat from his comfortable vacation, like I were a struggling father Dustin Hoffman might play in an Oscar-hoping role, and bring him to his new home. He'll at first be unsure, but then he'll start with the sniffing, and sniffing his own ass, and sniffing some more, and then decide to plop down in the sun of his, of our, new window. I'll be pitching in again, to society—how else would people find these patios, or know what to order, or know ahead of time what to expect from the ambience? I'll save some bucks, too, once the editor—speed gun of soul—deems my happiness and self-worth acceptable, and sends a check.

Aside from the short residency back home, where I'm letting Mom's spaghetti and meatballs, the freezer's frozen *taquitos*, and late nights with a displaced cat in a suburban basement with a nice TV ease the return from Grandma's and Mighty Taco, I'm also in a semi, near-amicable hiatus from X. We both know there's nothing there, but we're being nice to ourselves, like adults learn to do, there no longer any question that we're letting it dissolve. Like so much stomach-assuaging Pepto.

I feel I've forgotten the ability of the world to surprise, and I'm actually having a hard time getting over this pizza. It's all too much, bursting flavors, char spots on the edges of crust, doughy soft in the middle, tomatoes from the old country, curdy and stretchy fresh mozz. At one point I even think about ordering a glass of wine, but instead find myself asking for another beer, then pontificating.

"Yeah," I say, "even I'm changing. Look, Pepto." I pat my stomach.

Smoke gives me a look. "You know that's Alka-Seltzer, right? You don't dissolve Pepto in water."

"Whatever. Mother-loving Sopressaaatttaaaa. See, I'm trying new things!"

"You're still gonna watch the fucking Comeback Game this weekend at some point and you know it!"

"Well, I mean, it's almost Thurman's birthday, so yeah, of course…"

Soon, like good things go, it's over and we're rehashing the meal. Smoke is satisfied, rubbing his gut, rubbing the back of his head, smoking covertly, holding the butt down under his seat, puffing hard and heavy when the waitress is out of sight, like it's his last chance and he's getting giddy with forgotten food friendship and a night out. The release of a domesticated man, now with the prospect of getting real drunk and Paul Simon-soundtracked chummy. He keeps jumping back to New Orleans, like he used to, all those nights ago, on the roof, with the world under us and the cigarettes endless and the biggest responsibility the one that came when we were done with the beers we were drinking and one of us would have to trudge down the stairs and back up with fresh ones. He's planning our next trip there, my next book, an article I should write, the point not entirely clear.

"Smoke, you're telling me all signposts of the culture, and the town's resilience after the storm, can be gleaned from the explosion of fresh beignet powder?"

He waves that off. "You're not listening. The *soft* explosion of beignet powder." He shakes his head, as if to say *some people*, like I'm an idiot. "It's so sooooofffffft…"

"And that's the article? I pitch that to the editor?"

"Yeah! Or just do another po' boy piece, fuck, I don't care. When's the book come out? Let's get down there on tour!"

"Ok, well, first, will you at least read this piece?"

"I'll scan it. Well, the pictures. I'll scan the pictures, for sure."

"You're a good friend."

"And you're a good fat fuck hack writer!"

"That means a lot, Smoke. And can you do me one more thing?"

"Sorry, man, first drink at the next place is on you."

"Ok. Can you just leave a comment?"

"Like…?"

"Proustian."

"You want me to write a comment on your patio piece and say that it's Proustian?"

"Yeah."

"And that means…?"

"That's it's fucking dope."

The waitress whisks away the bill, annoyed with us, us not caring, noisily clamoring the plastic seats against the concrete as we rise up and out, toward later night things. She doesn't notice, doesn't care herself, definitely doesn't do the thing I'm still waiting for, where somebody will run my debit card, look down, notice the name, look up, and say, "Aren't you…" It will be a pretty blonde, one studying writing at Depaul, and she'll tell me how much my thoughts on garlic have meant to her, and she'll ask if I might want to go for some tacos and read poetry and then fuck. Of course it won't happen, not this time, certainly, the pizzas for my assignment going straight to Smoke's credit card. My wallet is rife with cash from Grandma, and a bit more from Mom, and the promise has been laid clear, enunciated with a sweep of the hand, to spend it all, but we both realize the night isn't even young yet.

Later, we're going through everything that happened since the last time we comforted each other over beers. The night grows dark as we cross Lincoln, and we're not talking about it but we know we're heading toward Delilah's, saddling up, the hour still too early for a crowd, how we like it. Whiskeys for us both, neat this time, easing digestion, and I'm warming toward Smoke, and the possibility of a not-too-cold April night with a hint of rain loosening us away from self-preservation, me from my predilection to direct conversation away from anything about me. I feel sturdy enough to go toward the Bills, even.

"So everybody was pissed at each other, why?" Smoke asks.

"Because they lost?"

I haven't run through the entire brawl with anyone yet, the dropped pizza a bridge too far, enough to necessitate deflection, jokes, levity in the face of sadness. Johnny and I have hardly mentioned it, averted conversations, it being too soon, too much.

"No, that's the thing. This is *before* the game."

I flash on everybody, a sudden coursing energy, Ike like a bull in China, as they say, and I recall some blood, much spilled red sauce, at least one black eye, Grandma almost getting taken out by the swirling mass of negative Bills game day energy. A simple push for .500, and for some pizza to go along with it; to gather for one last time, before Christmas, and get drunk and let the toilet flush on our days in Buffalo.

I'm trying to explain the run-up, embarrassed for us, for myself, struggling for the words, writer's block in bar conversation. "You know…shit, didn't you ever have a family?" I put my arms out to the side, a *life is fucked* gesticulation.

"Yeah. Family shit." Smoke nods. "I get it, I get it."

He doesn't quite, though, so I continue. "Well, yeah, but did you have family during Super Bowl 25?"

"Teddy…"

"As a Bills fan?"

By the time we've moved to the beer-and-shot portion of the evening, he's beginning an attempt at sympathy, or placation.

"Really, though, I can't believe they lost that game." There's a part that's compassionate, tender, discussing the recent flailing end to another losing season, but another part, with his other hand, is reaching out to thrust a sword into my kidneys.

"Eh, 7-9 ain't so bad. Almost .500. And Jackson's still got one year left, with his ACL intact, motherfucker!"

With this, we tink glasses, let out smiles, know together that, no matter what brutalities and realities of the world find us, and no matter the long gaps in-between them, we'll be back at it, this charade of disappointment and drinking through Sunday letdowns, next season.

"So you did end up watching it?" he asks, disbelieving.

"Yeah."

"Even after the throat punches and the cops came and everything?"

"Yeah, they were pretty understanding."

"Can't believe you didn't get arrested."

"Oh, we did."

"What!? Yeah?"

"But I explained, to the sergeant, you know? About the pizza."

"And?"

"He understood. Tension. Outrage. Fucker was from Orchard Park."

"So, you got out in time, and watched it?" He shakes his head and takes a sip, gazing off, then more shaking, then another sip. "Where'd you watch it?"

"Watched it at Helka's, with Johnny. And Ike."

A final image flashes of the four of us. Helka is wearing a '92 AFC Championship sweatshirt with drops of red down the front, silently sitting in her chair with legs crossed, small again, quiet; Johnny won't take his chin from his hand, shielding the right side of his face from us, occasionally testing the tenderness of an area just under his jaw; there's a tissue in my nose, and a gentle daze upon my face, and I'm working my tongue against my front teeth, not sure if they've always felt like that, seismic somehow; Ike seems mostly fine, just coughing a bit now and then, like he's worked out, worked something out, his hair sticking up just a touch, a newfound weight tugging at the left of his lower lip, keeping it down. Occasionally he picks up his right hand, as if to say something with it, opening his palm, releasing air inside, and then lowering it back to his side. O.G. Johnny's face is turned toward the TV, all in, no matter what, no turning around, no turning back, the final game of the season, one last huzzah, or something.

"You want a beer?" Ike asks, to no one in particular.

"The fuck kinda question is that?" Johnny and I answer, in unison, and Ike ambles off to the kitchen, miming Helka's octogenarian shuffle, a resigned smile about the room when he brings back four cans of Genesee.

By the middle of the third quarter, the three of us were home, waiting for the pizza guy—a *new* pizza guy—and the Bills were losing.

EPILOGUE

CHICAGO (0-0)

"Glad and Sorry" plays on the juke, the piano's *dah dah dah dah* echoing about the nervous noon-ish energy. Glasses tink around the bar, lots of them, and every possible varietal of football jersey litters the room: Cincinnati, Detroit, a blonde in a low-cut Dolphins number, even a bona fide Cleveland fan over in one corner, checking his phone, for hope.

But, most prominently, most obscene, is the glut of Bills jerseys dominating a reserved side section. There's a Thurman, looking classic; more than a few Jacksons, in different colors; you wonder why anyone would buy a Kelso, but then you see one and it looks so cool, and in white, no less. It's the kickoff to a new season, and our humble Milwaukee Avenue sports consulate has seemingly been overtaken by Buffalo expats. There's something vaguely Manson-ish about the proceedings, strangers greeting strangers with hugs, special high-fives being invented on the fly, an old guy with a gray mustache assuming the mentor roll, his arm around a young bearded dude with skinny pants, a few black guys in Timberlands and straight brims, an Indian-looking young couple, and everybody talking about when they got out, their favorite spot for fish frys, which Mighty Taco was closest to their old home.

I'm taking it in by degrees, with a weird grin and scrunched eyebrows, talking to the one guy in a Simpson 32 jersey.

"What is this you started? A cult?"

"Well…" Dustin smiles. "We don't use the C-word."

He bursts into deep laughter, his volume amplified, his blood pressure palpable. His smile too feels heightened, radiant, extra toothy as he makes a sweeping gesture with his hand around the room, as if to say something like, "And lo…" like it's biblical times.

He's nodding to himself, repeatedly, and to me, like a gentle elbow nudge, an "Ehhh?" with all due satisfaction, this his greatest work, a mobilized community of alcoholics and four-time losers, a support group with a drinking problem laid in front of the two of us like some kind of unholy kingdom of survivors and smokers and chicken wing guts. We even have our own waitress.

I'm finishing my standard pre-game pale ale and shot of Powers, cooling nerves, sitting on a stool by the edge of the circle, my back and elbows leaning against the bar, still shaking my head, nursing my two-drink start to a many-drink day, feeling winded from the cavalcade of handshakes and Buffalo-area burg conversational sling shots.

"You're from Tonawanda!? Fuck! Holy shit, Al! This dude's from Tonawanda!"

"No fucking shit, I'm from *North* Tonawanda!"

Pervasive, undulating, is the head-scratching feel of traveling all the way around the world to end up next door.

"Make a sports play!" The cry comes at once and through the cognitive cobwebs, chesty and desperate over our heads as the waitress scoots by with another tray of Labatts—new to the menu, for us, for Dustin—echoing around the room that is echoing itself with talking heads dissecting the rest of Sunday's potentialities. And, as if in answer, the Bills win the coin toss, setting Dustin off on a wave of high-fiving everyone in our group, and even some nearby Bears fans, calm and somewhat amused by the Buffalo-born madness taking their bar by storm.

"Who needs a shot!?" Dustin yells, pacing a bit, on his third beer as we continue getting caught up, him wanting to hear everything about every detail, every meal in Buffalo, though we've done this before, multiple times throughout the summer. I want to move to another part of the room, need to see some blood on the field, some catharsis, but then, because it's been a while, and because he still feels bad, he gets sheepish a bit, apologizing for the way my hands hurt, cut by the corrugation, after my stabby attempt at real work.

"Speaking of work, have I got the idea for your book," he says, and like that we're over particulars and I'm grateful, ready for rhetoricals, theoreticals, fantasies, bullshit.

"Yeah, well, the book. Thing is, I kind of already wrote it."

"No, no, no, your next book."

The notion hadn't occurred to me, but then, like a man remembering the very keys he's looking for are in his hand, I realize there are somehow more empty pages available in Microsoft Word.

"Yeah? And...?" I'm rolling with it, ready.

"Let the bad guy win."

"Let the bad guy win?"

"Let the bad guy," Dustin stops, takes a considerable swill, "win."

"Norwood?"

"Sure. Yeah. Let Norwood win."

"But is he the bad guy?"

"The bad good guy. It's a paradox. Very literary."

Like that, struck dumb and looking very much the part of the mouth-breather, all *well I never taught of dat before*, bean-hole agape, I'm pondering the book. The next book. Like the dawning of some revolutionary concept, the peach and the Proust moment, I consider making this one *good*. Readable, how about? A splicing thing of food and culture and bad guy redemption. Or just straight up bad guy-ness. The meat running with the cheese, the rivulets therein, caloric description of the type never before seen, not since, no, not even then. Food as a beating heart, or the blood for the heart. A body metaphor, something, whatever, I'll fix it in editing. From this sunny Sunday bar spot, sober work therein and empty pages far enough away from the now, it seems, feels, worth it. Celebrate Norwood. Dedicate it to Norwood.

"Dustin, I'm impressed. I've taught you so much of literature."

"Everything I know, bro. E-ver-eee-thing."

I'm instantly in quick flashback, everybody from before, all of us, Ike, Helka, Johnny, our old man looking for the back door on all this, because of the straw that broke the horse's back, as they say, because of a missed field goal. On the lonely nights we've all spent looking for something at the bottom of a bottle, or on the waiting for someone to ring the doorbell and tell us everything, or, at the very least, "Here's your pizza," us always seeking answers beneath such deep, shimmering pools of wing sauce. I think of how we all got to this place because of the faulty foot actions of one rushed bad guy.

But at least we have our reason, our plot synopsis, laid out nice and neat, our scar and badge of honor clear, just needing an outline and a few years of inspired keyboard dawdling. It's about a bad man needing his comeuppance, or a handshake, or one of those really hard, somewhat-nefarious handshakes, where you don't let go, make it awkward, stare deep into eyes with controlled malevolence and then start to squeeze harder, until the forefinger and pinky start shifting noticeably toward one another.

Dustin is circling the room, high-fiving everyone, baby-high-fiving with his big calloused mitt a Bills baby that, in full galloping Buffalo onesie, is seated in a car seat on a table next to some beers. And now Dustin is high-kneeing in place, putting his hands on his head, punching the top of his stool, and I'm feeling a laugh come on, a valve, a release, and he seems to remember something, and points at my near-empty pint glass with questioning eyes. I nod, but he is already moving toward the bar, no time to wait for our waitress, not with so much nervous vigor sizzling, like an overheated pan of bacon grease. He's showing, pointing the way, with a mimed stiff arm and a smile on his face, and on his way to the tender, 20 firmly in hand, Dustin, with grave beer-buying purpose, making the ultimate of sports plays, heartily slaps me on the back and, from down in his gut, says, "I got you."

And it's almost time for kickoff.

www.ingramcontent.com/pod-product-compliance
Lightning Source LLC
Chambersburg PA
CBHW020647260626
47157CB00008B/2942